TIMELESS ALPHA

VAIBHAV VIJAY RATNAPARKHI

INDIA • SINGAPORE • MALAYSIA

ISBN 979-8-89067-784-6

Contents

Chapter 1

The Great Departure

The night was dark, its obsidian depth only broken by the stars, yet the stars shone like a myriad of tiny diamonds scattered across the vast canvas of the sky. As I rolled down the car window, I was greeted by a breeze that was surprisingly gentle and soothing. The memories of my past, the choices I'd made, all seemed to swirl around me. The wind, it felt like an old friend, offering solace. It was as if the wind itself was trying to comfort me, to ease the heavy burden that weighed on my heart. The night whispered secrets, its air thick with the scent of the Deccan Plateau's unique flora, a mix of earthy, spicy fragrances that had become familiar to me over the years. The weight of my past pressed heavily on me as I sped forward, trying to outrun it, escaping from a life that had become unbearable. The familiar route from Pune to Mumbai had always been a journey of routine, either for work or leisure. But tonight, it felt different, charged with urgency and desperation. The journey from Pune to Mumbai was one I had made many times before, but never under circumstances like these. As the city lights of Pune gradually receded in the rear-view mirror, with every passing moment, the reflections of my past grew clearer, each more haunting than the last, on the life I was leaving behind – the crushing corporate job, the failed relationships, the mounting debts. Each milestone that passed seemed to carry away with it a piece of my past. I understood my decision to flee was not the right one. Escapism is often seen as a coward's choice, a refusal to face one's problems. But in my case, it felt like the only option left. It was either this or the unthinkable alternative - ending my own life. Mauritius had been a dream destination for a while, a haven often painted in my mind during my darkest hours. It was a relatively inexpensive place to live, and with the money I had saved up, I could live there comfortably, maintaining my dignity and self-respect. The thought of the turquoise waters and the tranquil beaches was a beacon of hope, a promise of a fresh start. Suddenly, my heart skipped a beat as I saw the flashing lights of a police checkpoint up ahead. The pulsating lights seemed to synchronize with the thumping in my chest, a rhythm of dread. I knew I had to act normal, to hide the turmoil that was churning inside me. Drinking and driving is a serious offense in India, and I had had a few drinks to steel my nerves for the journey. But at that moment, it did not matter to me. I was leaving this country, leaving everything behind. The police officer approached my car, his stern face illuminated by the harsh glare of the checkpoint lights. "Young man, I need to see your driving license, PUC papers, and insurance papers," he demanded. His voice echoed in my ears, bringing me back to the reality of the situation. I fumbled in my pocket and handed him what I thought was my license. He looked at it and then back at me, a hint of amusement in his eyes. "This is your voter ID, not your driving license. Shinde, bring the Breathalyzer. And who is this young boy?" he asked, peering into the backseat of my car. I turned around, my heart pounding in my chest. To my utter shock, there was a young man sitting in the backseat. He was fair-skinned, with a light beard and a well-maintained military-style haircut. His clothes suggested that he came from a wealthy family. My mind raced with questions, my palms sweating on the steering wheel. Who was he? How had he gotten into my car? What did he want? As I struggled to make sense of the situation, the young man placed his hand on my shoulder. "Don't worry, I'm here to help you," he said, his voice calm and reassuring. His touch was strangely comforting, like a balm on my frayed nerves. I did not know what to say or do. I was about to be caught in a Breathalyzer test, and yet, this stranger was telling me not to worry. As the police officer was distracted by a phone call, the young man, with a conspiratorial glance at me, advised me to tell the truth. My throat felt dry as I swallowed hard, mustering the courage to confess to the officer that I had been drinking. To my surprise, he let me go without imposing any fine. It felt like a stroke of luck, the first one I had had in a long time. Once we were safely away from the checkpoint, I pulled over to the side of the road. The silence of the night was punctuated by the ticking of the car's engine, its rhythm matching my racing heartbeat. I turned to face the stranger; my mind filled with questions. "Who are you? How did you get into my car?" I demanded. He just smiled at me, a warm, friendly smile that somehow put me at ease. "My name is Kriyansh," he said. "I'm a space scientist. I was on my way to Mumbai from Lonavla when I was attacked by some anti-social elements. I had to hide in your car. Thank you for giving me a lift."

"But how do you know my name?" I asked, puzzled. "That's not important," he replied. "What's important is why you're running away." And so, our journey continued, two strangers bound by circumstances, heading towards an uncertain future. Little did I know then that this journey would take us not just to Mumbai, but beyond the confines of time and space itself. The road hummed beneath the wheels of my car as we navigated the serpentine path down the Deccan Plateau. The inky blackness of the night was marred only by the fleeting beams of our headlights. The air was dense with the familiar smell of damp earth, interspersed with the crisp, metallic scent of rain on the tarmac. The trees looming on either side of the road formed an arch, their leaves whispering ancient secrets in the wind. I stole a glance at Kriyansh through the rearview mirror. He was staring out the window, his pale blue eyes reflecting the spectral dance of moonlight on the rain-splattered windowpane. His jaw was set, a stark contrast to the softness of his features, and his lips were a thin line, revealing nothing of his thoughts. His accent was light, laced with a hint of an unplaceable foreign accent. It was evident that he was well-educated and well-travelled. Yet, there was an air of mystery about him, something enigmatic that drew me in. The silence between us was comfortable, interrupted only by the occasional patter of raindrops on the roof of the car. Kriyansh broke the silence, his voice a melodious baritone that soothed my frayed nerves, "Yash, you've made a brave decision, a decision that most people wouldn't dare to make. Running away is not always an act of cowardice. Sometimes, it is an act of survival, an act of self-preservation. It's the first step towards finding oneself."

His words hung in the air, stirring up a whirlwind of emotions within me. It was as if he had read my mind, understood my turmoil, and voiced my innermost fears and hopes. I glanced at him again, his serene face bathed in the soft glow of the car's interior lights. His presence was strangely comforting, his words resonating with my own thoughts. We crossed the city limits and entered the realm of the countryside. The rain had eased into a gentle drizzle, the pitter-patter of droplets on the leaves creating a symphony of its own. The tall, imposing buildings gave way to small, thatched huts, their inhabitants fast asleep. The moon, now clear of the clouds, cast an ethereal glow on the landscape, making the paddy fields look like a sea of silver. The occasional hoot of an owl, the rustling of leaves, and the distant bark of a dog were the only sounds that punctuated the night. Suddenly, a pair of eyes gleamed in the headlights. A deer had wandered onto the road. With a swift maneuverer, I managed to avoid hitting it. My heart pounded in my chest as I brought the car to a halt. Kriyansh, surprisingly unruffled, turned to me and said, "Well, that was close, wasn't it? But do not worry, Yash. You are a good driver. And remember, every journey has its obstacles. It's how we navigate them that matters." His words, though meant to comfort me, served as a stark reminder of the obstacles that lay ahead. I was leaving my old life behind, venturing into uncharted territories. But Kriyansh's calm demeanour and the inexplicable faith he had in me gave me the strength to carry on. As we resumed our journey, the first rays of dawn began to pierce the night sky. The world was slowly waking up, the darkness giving way to the light. The road ahead was long and winding, but I was no longer alone. I had Kriyansh by my side, a stranger who had become my confidante, my guide. I was filled with a sense of hope and anticipation, ready to face whatever lay ahead. Little did I know then, that this journey was just the beginning of an adventure that would take us beyond the realms of the imaginable. The silence in the car was thick, pregnant with unsaid words and unasked questions. The soft hum of the car's engine and the occasional patter of the rain were the only sounds that accompanied us. As I drove, my mind wandered back to the life I was leaving behind. I thought about the countless nights

I had spent tossing and turning, unable to find peace. The relentless pressure at work, the staggering debts, the feeling of being trapped in a life that was not my own. The loneliness that had enveloped me, even amid a crowd. The crippling anxiety that had gnawed at me, day in and day out. The hopelessness that had driven me to the edge, forcing me to contemplate the unthinkable. Yet here I was, fleeing from it all, hoping to disappear and start anew. It was a desperate gamble, a leap of faith. But it was the only way out I could see. And now, I had Kriyansh, a stranger, accompanying me on this journey. His presence, though unexpected, was oddly comforting. His calm demeanour and insightful words were like a balm to my troubled mind. However, as the miles rolled by, a nagging thought kept gnawing at me. Who was Kriyansh? What were his intentions? Why had he chosen to help me? Was it just a random act of kindness, or was there more to it than met the eye? His enigmatic smile and cryptic words hinted at a deeper story. His composed demeanour and the ease with which he had handled the situation at the police checkpoint suggested that he was no ordinary person. And his claim of being a space scientist only added to the mystery. As I pondered over these questions, Kriyansh's voice broke through my thoughts. "Yash," he said, his voice low and serious, "I can see that you're struggling. I understand that you are going through a tough time. But remember, every dark night is followed by a dawn. Do not lose hope. Sometimes, running away is not a sign of weakness, but a sign of strength. It takes courage to let go of the familiar and step into the unknown."

His words echoed in my mind, sparking a glimmer of hope. Perhaps, this journey, as uncertain and daunting as it was, was a step towards a new beginning. A chance to break free from the shackles of my past and start afresh. Maybe, just maybe, I could find the peace I had been longing for. As the sun began to peek over the horizon, bathing the world in a warm, golden light, I could not help but feel a sense of anticipation. With Kriyansh by my side, I was ready to face whatever lay ahead. Little did I know that this journey would not only lead me to a new life but also reveal secrets that would shatter the boundaries of my reality.

The events of the night had taken a toll on Yash, both physically and mentally. The unexpected encounter with the police, the stranger in his car, and the revelations about time travel were more than he had anticipated. As they continued their journey, the night's silence was punctuated only by the hum of the car's engine and the occasional call of nocturnal creatures. Yash felt his eyelids grow heavy, and he could sense sleep beckoning him.

Before he could give in to the fatigue, Kriyansh's voice pulled him back. "Yash, remember that sometimes, the universe has its own way of guiding us, even if the path is unclear. Tonight, our paths have intertwined for a reason, and together, we will navigate the journey ahead." Yash nodded, taking solace in Kriyansh's words. The weight of his past still lingered, but now there was a glimmer of hope on the horizon. As the first light of dawn began to paint the sky, Yash felt a sense of anticipation. A new day, a new beginning, and a journey that promised to be unlike any other.

Chapter 2

The Revelation and the Journey Through Time

With the breaking of dawn, Yash was awakened from his reverie. The early morning sun streamed through the car windows, casting a golden hue on everything. As he rubbed his eyes, adjusting to the light, the events of the previous night came flooding back. The stranger, Kriyansh, and his mind-boggling revelations about time travel. Yash looked over at him, trying to discern more about this mysterious man who had suddenly become an integral part of his life.

Kriyansh, sensing Yash's gaze, smiled warmly. "Good morning, Yash. I hope you're ready for the day. Today, we embark on a journey, not just through space but through time. But before we dive into the mysteries of the universe, let's address the questions clouding your mind." Yash nodded, eager to unravel the enigma that was Kriyansh. As the car sped on, a tale of cosmic wonders, timeless adventures, and the intricate dance of fate and destiny began to unfold.

As the car hummed along the highway, the cityscape of Mumbai slowly fading into the distance, Yash found himself drawn into the enigma that was Kriyansh. The calmness that Kriyansh exuded, his inexplicable knowledge of Yash's name, and his sudden, almost magical appearance in the car, all these elements stirred a whirlpool of questions in Yash's mind. Sensing the turmoil within Yash, Kriyansh decided it was time to unveil the truth. "I am not just a space scientist, Yash," Kriyansh began, his voice as steady as the rhythm of the car's engine. "I am also known by another name - Krishna."

The revelation hit Yash like a bolt from the blue. He turned to look at Kriyansh, his eyes wide with disbelief. He half-expected Kriyansh to burst into laughter, to tell him that it was all a joke. But the serene expression on Kriyansh's face, the earnestness in his eyes, told him that this was no jest. "But why are you here, in my car?" Yash managed to ask, his voice barely more than a whisper, his mind struggling to process the information. "I am here to help you, Yash," Kriyansh replied, his voice imbued with a warmth that seemed to soothe Yash's agitated mind. "I am aware of your struggles, your depression, your suicidal thoughts. I can guide you towards the answers you seek, but for that, we need to journey back in time."

Yash was sceptical, his rational mind rebelling against the idea. But he was also desperate, his soul yearning for a respite from the relentless torment of his life. He found himself nodding in agreement, ready to embark on this improbable journey, hoping against hope that it would lead him to a path of salvation. As the car sped along the highway, the city lights of Mumbai now just a distant glow, Kriyansh began to elucidate the concept of time travel. He spoke of wormholes, of quantum physics, of the space-time continuum, his words painting a picture of a universe far more complex and mysterious than Yash had ever imagined. But most of his explanations flew over Yash's head, his mind too preoccupied with the tantalizing prospect of escaping his present life and finding solace in the past. Before they embarked on their temporal voyage, Yash felt a compelling need to unburden his soul. He began to talk about his life, his struggles, his failures. His words flowed like a torrent, carrying with them the pain and despair that had been his constant companions. He spoke of his crumbling marriage, his unfulfilling job, his incessant battles with depression. He talked about the daily altercations with his wife Isha, a woman of sharp features and a sharper tongue. Her once loving brown eyes had turned cold and distant over the years, her once comforting presence now a source of constant anxiety. He talked about the disappointment he saw in his parents' eyes, Gautam and Vedika. His father Gautam, a tall and sturdy man with a gruff exterior hiding a soft heart, his eyes always carrying a hint of sadness whenever they met Yash's. His mother Vedika, a petite woman with a radiant smile that had lost its shine over the years, her constant worry for Yash visible in her tired eyes. He spoke of the relentless pressure from his boss Naksh Sharma, a suave man of intimidating stature, his dark eyes always scrutinizing, always judging. The once motivational leader had now become a symbol of dread in Yash's life. He mentioned his strained relationship with his in-laws, Manoj and Divya. Manoj, a man of few words but sharp intellect, his stern gaze and strict demeanour always making Yash uncomfortable. Divya, a woman of grace and poise, her soft-spoken nature hiding a judgmental side that often-left Yash feeling inadequate. He laid bare his feelings of worthlessness, his contemplation of suicide, his desperate longing for an end to his suffering. His last wish was to hug his parents and apologize for not taking a stand when they needed him the most. Kriyansh listened in silence, his eyes reflecting a deep understanding and empathy. "Yash," he finally said, "all these problems, these struggles, they are part of your journey. But they do not define you. And they are not insurmountable. Remember, every problem has a solution, every question has an answer. And sometimes, to find those answers, we need to look beyond our present circumstances."

His words hung in the air, a beacon of hope in the darkness that had enveloped Yash's life. With renewed determination, they continued their journey, the city lights of Mumbai now a mere speck in the rearview mirror. As they delved deeper into the mysteries of time and the wisdom of the past, Yash could not help but feel a glimmer of hope. Perhaps this journey, as improbable as it seemed, would lead him to the answers he sought, to the peace he craved. As the hours passed, Kriyansh delved deeper into the intricacies of time travel. He explained how time, like space, was a dimension that could be navigated. He spoke of the theory of relativity, of how time could be bent and twisted, creating pathways to different eras. He talked about the role of gravity, of how massive objects could warp the fabric of space-time, creating wormholes that could serve as shortcuts through time. Yash listened, his skepticism slowly giving way to fascination. The idea of time travel, once a mere figment of science fiction, was now a tangible possibility. He found himself drawn into Kriyansh's narrative, his mind opening to the limitless possibilities that lay ahead. As they neared their destination, Kriyansh turned to Yash. "Are you ready, Yash?" he asked, his eyes gleaming with anticipation. Yash took a deep breath, his heart pounding in his chest. He was about to embark on a journey beyond his wildest dreams, a journey that could change his life forever. "I'm ready," he replied, his voice steady, his resolve unwavering. With a nod of approval, Kriyansh turned his attention back to the road, the car speeding towards their destination, towards the beginning of their incredible journey through time. As the daylight slowly gave way to twilight, the car was suffused with the warm, orange glow of the setting sun. The horizon was a riot of colors, the setting sun painting the sky with shades of red, orange, and purple. The air was heavy with the scent of the sea, the breeze carrying with it the salty tang that was unmistakably Mumbai. Yash glanced at Kriyansh, still struggling to wrap his mind around the incredible revelations of the day. Kriyansh, sensing his bewilderment, turned to him with a reassuring smile, "I know, Yash. The concept of time travel is a hard pill to swallow. But trust me, it's not as complicated as it sounds."

Kriyansh delved into the science of time travel, his words interspersed with the jargon of quantum physics and astrophysics. He spoke about Einstein's Theory of Relativity, about wormholes and black holes, about the space-time continuum and quantum entanglement. His words painted a picture of a universe that was far more complex and awe-inspiring than anything Yash could have ever imagined. Yash listened with rapt attention; his skepticism gradually replaced by a sense of wonder. His mind raced with questions, the possibilities of time travel opening a whole new world of possibilities. "But Kriyansh," he asked, "where would we go? What point in time would we travel to?"

Kriyansh turned to him, his eyes twinkling with mischief. "That, Yash," he said, "is entirely up to you. The past, the present, the future - they are all at your disposal. All you need to do is make a choice." Yash was taken aback. He had the power to choose, the power to decide his own destiny. It was a daunting prospect, but it was also an opportunity, a chance to change the course of his life. After a moment of contemplation, he made his choice. "I want to travel to the future," he said, his voice steady, his decision firm. Kriyansh raised his eyebrows in surprise. "The future, eh?" he mused. "That's an unusual choice. Most people would choose to travel to the past, to right their wrongs or relive their happiest moments. But the future...that's a whole new ball game." Despite his surprise, Kriyansh did not question Yash's choice. He respected it, understanding that every person had their own reasons, their own motivations. "Very well, Yash," he said, his tone serious. "If the future is what you seek, then the future it shall be."

As the twilight gave way to the darkness of the night, the car continued to hum along the highway, the cityscape of Mumbai now nothing more than a distant memory. Yash found himself lost in thought, his mind filled with a strange sense of anticipation and apprehension. He was about to embark on a journey unlike any other, a journey that could change his life forever. Kriyansh's voice brought him back to reality. "Remember, Yash," he said, "time travel is not just a physical journey. It is also a journey of the mind, a journey of self-discovery. It is an opportunity to learn, to grow, to evolve. And who knows, you might just find the answers you've been looking for."

His words hung in the air, a beacon of hope in the darkness of uncertainty. As the car sped along the highway, the city lights of Mumbai now nothing more than a faint glow in the distance, Yash couldn't help but feel a sense of exhilaration. He was about to embark on an adventure of a lifetime, an adventure that could very well change the course of his life. "I'm ready, Kriyansh," he said, his voice filled with determination. "Let's do this."

With a nod of approval, Kriyansh pressed a button on the dashboard. Suddenly, the car was enveloped in a blinding light. The roar of the engine was drowned out by a deafening hum. The world outside the car started to blur, the scenery morphing into a whirlpool of colors. And then, just as suddenly as it had begun, the light faded, the hum died down, and the car came to a halt. Yash looked around, his heart pounding in his chest. The cityscape of Mumbai was gone. In its place was a futuristic metropolis, its skyscrapers reaching up to the sky, its streets buzzing with hover cars and drones. Yash turned to Kriyansh, his eyes wide with amazement. "We did it," he said, his voice filled with awe. "We actually did it. We travelled through time." Kriyansh smiled, his eyes sparkling with satisfaction. "Yes, Yash," he said. "Welcome to the future. Welcome to your future."

Amid the strange, futuristic metropolis, the car sat like an anachronism from a bygone era. Yash gazed out of the window in awe, his eyes scanning the alien landscape that was supposedly his future. The neon-lit skyscrapers towered above, their sharp, geometric designs contrasting with the fluid, almost organic architecture of the lower buildings. Hover cars darted between the buildings, their lights leaving streaks of colour against the dark sky. Drones flitted about like oversized fireflies, their wings humming softly as they went about their tasks. “Where are we?” Yash asked, his voice barely above a whisper. He half-expected Kriyansh to reveal that it was all a dream, a figment of his imagination. But the surreal cityscape outside was as tangible as the car seat beneath him. “This, Yash,” Kriyansh said with a hint of pride, “is Mumbai in the year 2100.”

Yash sat stunned, his mind struggling to reconcile the familiar name with the unfamiliar sight before his eyes. Mumbai, the city of dreams, the city he had left behind, had transformed into a vision from a science fiction movie. “It’s... it’s incredible,” he finally managed to say. As they drove through the city, Yash was struck by the harmony between technology and nature. Lush green vertical gardens adorned the exteriors of the buildings, their verdant foliage a stark contrast to the steel and glass structures. Artificial water bodies glistened under the city lights; their surfaces dotted with floating platforms that served as recreational spaces. The air was clean and fresh, a far cry from the polluted air of his time. Yash was so engrossed in the sights that he didn't notice the small robot that had approached the car. It was about the size of a basketball, its body adorned with flashing lights and spinning antennae. It hovered in front of the windshield, its mechanical eyes scanning the car. Yash jumped in surprise, but Kriyansh seemed unperturbed. "Don't worry, Yash," he said with a reassuring smile. "That's just a traffic drone. It's checking our registration."

Just as Kriyansh finished his sentence, the drone emitted a beep and floated away, evidently satisfied with what it had found. Yash let out a breath he didn't realize he had been holding. This future, with its advanced technology and unfamiliar norms, was overwhelming, to say the least. As they ventured deeper into the city, Kriyansh pointed out various landmarks and explained their significance. He showed Yash the solar highways that generated electricity, the autonomous hover taxis that reduced traffic congestion, and the smart buildings that adjusted their temperature and lighting according to the weather and occupancy. Despite the unfamiliarity, Yash found himself marvelling at the advancements. He couldn't help but wonder how much life must have improved with such developments. However, the thought was quickly overshadowed by a pressing concern. "Kriyansh," he asked, "how am I going to fit into this future? I don't know anything about this world."

Kriyansh turned to him; his eyes gleaming with reassurance. "Yash," he said, "remember that every journey starts with a single step. You will learn, you will adapt, and most importantly, you will grow. This is your future, and you have the power to shape it."

His words filled Yash with a sense of hope, a feeling he had almost forgotten. Perhaps this journey, as absurd and incredible as it seemed, was exactly what he needed. Perhaps this was his chance to start afresh, to escape the shackles of his past and embrace a new beginning. With this newfound optimism, Yash sat back in his seat, ready to face whatever this future had in store for him.

The whirl of emotions and confounding revelations had taken its toll on Yash, but he felt a newfound sense of purpose. As they drove further, the surroundings began to blur, and an eerie silence enveloped them. Yash could feel a tingling sensation, like a mild electric current coursing through his body. "Close your eyes, Yash. Focus on my voice. Let go of your present, and embrace the journey," Kriyansh whispered. Taking a deep breath, Yash closed his eyes. He heard Kriyansh chanting softly, the verses unfamiliar but soothing. The car's hum transformed into a rhythmic drone, harmonizing with Kriyansh's chants. Yash felt as if he was floating, untethered from the confines of the vehicle and the reality he knew.

Chapter 3

The Journey Begins - A Leap into the Past

When Yash opened his eyes, he was no longer in the car. The deafening sounds of battle cries and clashing metal surrounded him. The atmosphere was thick with dust and tension. The modern cityscape of Mumbai was replaced by a vast expanse of warriors, chariots, and elephants. Disoriented, Yash turned to find Kriyansh beside him, looking calm amid the chaos. "Welcome, Yash, to a pivotal moment in history. Welcome to the battlefield of Kurukshetra."

The city lights of Mumbai receded into the distance, swallowed by the enveloping darkness of the night. Yash felt the familiar grip of solitude, an introvert lost in his labyrinth of thoughts. He had always found solace in his own company, his mind a sanctuary where silence was a preferred companion over the world's relentless clamor. Yet, recently, this sanctuary felt more like a prison, its silence morphing into a suffocating solitude that echoed his failures and disappointments. Depression, an elusive phantom in the past, had insidiously seeped into his life, casting long, ominous shadows over his existence. It was like a persistent fog, obscuring the world around him and painting everything in a monochrome hue of despair. He felt like he was sinking into a bottomless abyss, each day a battle against his own mind. His gaze involuntarily shifted to Kriyansh, a stranger who had introduced himself as Krishna, the audacious guide who had promised him a journey towards the answers that seemed perpetually out of reach. Skepticism was Yash's initial reaction, a wall built by his scientific temperament and a staunch belief in logic. The proposition of time travel, of meeting characters from the epic Mahabharata, seemed as far-fetched as the fairy tales he had read as a child. But as he sat there, ensnared in the relentless grip of his miseries, he asked himself - what did he really have to lose? His once harmonious life was now a dissonant symphony of discord. His wife and parents were disillusioned, his boss treated him like a pawn, his friends had abandoned him, and his own mind was a hostile territory. If there was even a microscopic chance that this journey could salvage his life from its wreckage, he was ready to suspend his disbelief and take the leap of faith. "Alright, Kriyansh," Yash finally mustered the courage to say, his voice barely more than a whisper against the hum of the car's engine. "I'm ready to embark on this journey with you."

Kriyansh, who had maintained a serene silence until now, nodded and smiled, a gesture that somehow exuded an aura of reassurance. "Good," he responded, his voice a calm lullaby against the harsh reality of Yash's life. "Remember, Yash, this journey is not just about finding answers. It's also about finding yourself."

As Kriyansh pressed a button on his watch, the world outside started to warp and blur, like a painting caught in the rain. Yash felt a strange sensation, as if an invisible force was pulling him from all directions. His senses felt disjointed, reality slipping away like sand through his fingers. He closed his eyes, an instinctive response to brace himself for the plunge into the unknown. When he dared to open his eyes, he found himself in a world that was diametrically opposite to everything he knew. The comfort of his car had been replaced by the raw harshness of a battlefield. His ears were filled with the cacophony of war cries and clashing weapons. He saw warriors, their faces contorted with determination and fear, horses and elephants charging into the battlefield with a primal terror in their eyes, the sky turned into a canvas of arrows, and the sun, a silent spectator of the carnage below. Yash was a man of the 21st century, catapulted into an era where the currency of life was the edge of a sword. Fear washed over him, threatening to buckle his knees under its weight. But amidst this chaos and fear, he also felt a strange sense of exhilaration. He was in the epicenter of a story that had reverberated through the corridors of time, a story that had shaped the culture and philosophy of his land. Kriyansh's voice sliced through his thoughts, "Welcome to Kurukshetra, Yash," he said, his voice barely a whisper against the deafening din of the war. "Welcome to the past."

Yash, his mind a whirlpool of questions, turned to Kriyansh, but before he could voice his questions, Kriyansh silenced him with a raised hand. "There will be time for questions later, Yash," he said. "And in time, you will find your answers. But for now, let's focus on the task at hand."

And so, the journey into the past began, a journey that promised to transform Yash's life in unimaginable ways. Standing on the precipice of time, looking down at the battlefield of Kurukshetra, Yash felt a strange cocktail of awe, trepidation, and anticipation. He was about to dive into the labyrinth of time, a journey that would challenge his beliefs, test his courage, and potentially lead him to the answers he sought. As he stood on the battlefield, Yash had an unobstructed view of the panorama that was the Kurukshetra war, an event that held a prominent place in the annals of the Mahabharata. The battlefield reflected the grand conflict that had torn the kingdom apart. On one side of the field were the Pandavas, their army a sea of brave warriors. The Pandavas banner, a golden eagle against a field of blue, fluttered in the wind, a symbol of their unwavering determination to uphold dharma. Opposite them, stretching as far as Yash's eyes could see, was the army of the Kauravas. Their banner, a serpent coiled around a silver chakra, stood high against the crimson sky, a stark reminder of their ruthless quest for power. Between these two armies, the battlefield was a flurry of activity. Soldiers clashed with one another, their weapons singing a gruesome song of death and destruction. The air was filled with the sounds of war - the clang of steel against steel, the cries of wounded men, the neighing of terrified horses. Standing there, Yash could feel the raw energy of the battlefield. It was a stark contrast to the controlled environment of his IT job, a world away from the conference rooms and cubicles he was used to. It was a different kind of chaos, a chaos that was as terrifying as it was exhilarating. But even amidst the chaos, there was a sense of order, a method to the madness. The warriors, despite their ferocity, fought with honor, adhering to the codes of warfare. The charioteers navigated the battlefield with skill, avoiding the fallen and the wounded. The commanders, from their vantage points, directed their troops, their strategic acumen turning the tide of the battle. As he stood there, taking in the sights and sounds of the battlefield, Yash felt a surge of emotions. There was fear, of course, a primal fear of the violence and death that surrounded him. But there was also a sense of awe, a grudging respect for the warriors who fought with such courage and honor. And amidst it all, there was a spark of excitement, a thrill that coursed through his veins, a testament to the incredible journey he had embarked on. This was his past, a past that had shaped his culture, his beliefs, his very identity. As he stood on the battlefield of Kurukshetra, Yash felt a connection to his roots, a bond that transcended time and space. And in that moment, he knew that his journey into the past was just beginning, a journey that promised to be as enlightening as it was thrilling. As Yash stood on the battlefield of Kurukshetra, a thought struck him. He was supposed to be in the year 2100, wasn't he? That's what Kriyansh had said. But the scene before him was a far cry from what he had imagined the future would look like. He had pictured a world of advanced technology, of flying cars and towering skyscrapers, of robots and artificial intelligence. Instead, he found himself amidst a vast expanse of humans and animals, of swords and chariots, of dust and blood. It was like he had been thrown into a history textbook instead of a science fiction novel. "Kriyansh," Yash began, his voice barely audible over the din of the battlefield, "I thought you said we were going to the year 2100."

Kriyansh turned to look at him, a hint of amusement in his eyes. "I did say that, Yash," he replied, his voice calm and composed. "But I didn't specify which era of 2100 we would be visiting."

Yash blinked; confusion etched on his face. "Which era of 2100?" he echoed, his mind struggling to make sense of Kriyansh's words. Kriyansh nodded, a small smile playing on his lips. "Yes, Yash. Time is a complex construct. It's not as linear as we perceive it to be. There are multiple timelines, multiple possibilities. The future you envisioned, with its advanced technology and alien life forms, is just one of the many possibilities. The past we are in right now, the Kurukshetra war, is another."

Yash was silent for a moment, his mind racing to keep up with the information. "So, you're saying that we're in the year 2100, but in a different timeline?" he asked, hoping he had understood Kriyansh correctly. "Exactly," Kriyansh replied, his eyes gleaming with approval. "We're in a timeline where history repeats itself, where the events of the past play out again in the future. It's a cycle, Yash, a cycle of time."

Yash took a moment to process this. He had always been fascinated by the concept of time travel, by the idea of exploring different eras, of witnessing history unfold. But the reality of it was far more complex and intriguing than he had ever imagined. He was not just traveling through time; he was navigating through the myriad possibilities of existence, through the intricate tapestry of space-time. As he stood there, amidst the chaos and violence of the Kurukshetra war, Yash felt a strange sense of exhilaration. He was a part of something much bigger than himself, a part of a cosmic journey that transcended the boundaries of time and space. His problems, his failures, his disappointments, they all seemed insignificant in the grand scheme of things. He turned to Kriyansh, a newfound determination in his eyes. "I'm ready, Kriyansh," he declared, his voice steady and resolute. "I'm ready to embrace this journey, to seek the answers I've been looking for."

Kriyansh nodded, his eyes reflecting a similar determination. "Good," he said, his voice echoing over the sounds of the battlefield. "The journey is just beginning, Yash. And remember, it's not just about finding the answers. It's also about understanding the questions."

With that, they turned their attention back to the battlefield, their hearts filled with a strange mix of fear and excitement, their minds open to the infinite possibilities that lay ahead. They were time travelers, explorers of the cosmic sea, embarking on a journey that promised to change their lives in ways they could never have imagined. They were ready to face the challenges, to embrace the mysteries, to unravel the secrets of time. And as they stood there, on the cusp of their incredible journey, they knew that this was just the beginning. But in the heart of Yash, the darkness of doubt cast a long shadow. Would he find the answers he sought, or was he merely chasing shadows in a world veiled by time? The uncertainty of the journey weighed heavily on him, its suspense tugging at the edges of his resolve. As they ventured deeper into the labyrinth of time, the eerie silence of the unknown echoed around them, their path shrouded in an enigma that time alone could unravel.

Chapter 4

The Theatre of Timeless Wisdom - An Unfolding Odyssey

Standing on the consecrated grounds of Kurukshetra, Yash felt a surge of awe rush through his veins. The air around him seemed to hum with the echoes of ancient warfare, resonating with the timeless wisdom of the Bhagavad Gita. His heart pounded rhythmically in his chest, mimicking the relentless beat of a war drum, each beat amplifying the anticipation of an epic saga about to unfold. A tumult of emotions brewed within him - fear, awe, disbelief, curiosity - each one clamoring for dominance as he tried to comprehend the staggering sight sprawled before him. The battlefield, in its vastness, held an intimidating aura that was impossible to ignore. It stretched infinitely, like a canvas of time upon which the historic battle between the Pandavas and Kauravas was etched. The spectral armies, poised for a cataclysmic clash, seemed to be on the precipice of a war that would reverberate through the labyrinth of time. The air quivered with the cacophony of conch shells and war drums, each note a grim harbinger of the impending devastation, each beat a pulse in the burgeoning crescendo of war. Amidst this swirling chaos, Kriyansh was a beacon of tranquility. His serene presence amidst the ensuing tumult was akin to the calm eye of a hurricane. His eyes, the embodiment of age-old wisdom, reflected the infinite knowledge he had gathered over countless lifetimes. As the discordant symphony of the battlefield raged around them, Kriyansh's voice rang out, steady and clear. "Welcome to Kurukshetra, Yash," he said. His words, laden with gravity, hung heavy in the air, their profound significance resonating with the aura of the sacred grounds. "This is where the Bhagavad Gita was spoken, where Arjuna, besieged by his inner turmoil, found solace and guidance amidst the chaos of war."

His words stirred a whirlpool of questions in Yash's mind. "But why are we here, Kriyansh?" he asked, struggling to make himself heard over the deafening sounds of the battlefield. "What can I possibly learn from a war that unfolded thousands of years ago?"

Kriyansh's gaze remained fixed on the battlefield, his eyes reflecting the fire of the impending war. "You'd be surprised, Yash," he said, his voice laced with the wisdom of the ages. "The teachings of the Gita are timeless. They offer guidance for every facet of life, transcending the boundaries of time and space. They hold relevance even for the struggles you're currently facing." With these words, Kriyansh began to spin a yarn of tales, each thread spun from the wisdom of the Gita. He narrated the story of Arjuna, the mighty archer, whose martial prowess was unrivalled. Yet, even such a formidable warrior found himself shackled by doubt and fear on this battlefield. He stood torn between his duty as a warrior and his love for his kin, a predicament that resonated deeply with Yash's own internal conflicts. As Kriyansh recounted the tale, he painted a vivid picture of Arjuna - a man of commanding stature, his strong body honed by years of rigorous training. His eyes, usually calm, now reflected a storm of emotions. His normally steady hands trembled slightly, the weight of the decision he had to make weighing heavily on him. Kriyansh also shared the story of Dronacharya, the venerated guru of the Pandavas and Kauravas. He spoke of the day when Dronacharya asked his pupils to aim at a bird perched atop a distant tree. While others observed the tree, the sky, and the surroundings, Arjuna's sight was firmly fixed on the bird's eye - his target. This incident was a testament to Arjuna's unwavering focus and indomitable determination - qualities that Yash realized were integral to his own personal and professional growth. "Arjuna's focus wasn't just a testament to his archery skills, Yash," Kriyansh explained, his voice echoing with deep-seated conviction. "It was emblematic of his ability to concentrate on the task at hand, to not let his emotions or distractions divert him from his path. This is a lesson that holds relevance for you, Yash. Despite the turmoil that surrounds you, you must remain focused on your duties, on your dharma."

As Kriyansh's words washed over him, Yash felt a sense of tranquility settling within him. The tales of Arjuna and the teachings of the Gita began to resonate with him. He saw parallels between Arjuna's dilemmas and his own. He realized that his problems, much like Arjuna's, stemmed from his doubts and fears. Like Arjuna, he too needed to learn to focus, to carry out his duties without being swayed by his emotions. As the curtain of the first day ended, the battlefield was bathed in the soft, ethereal glow of the setting sun. The once-deafening sounds of the conch shells and war drums had faded into a haunting silence. The warriors retreated to their camps, mentally bracing themselves for the battles that lay ahead. As the sun dipped below the horizon, Yash found himself eagerly awaiting the lessons the morrow would bring. Little did he know that his journey into the past was just beginning, and that the lessons he would imbibe would irrevocably alter the course of his life. Days slipped into nights, and nights into days, marking the relentless passage of time. Under Kriyansh's guidance, Yash delved deeper into the teachings of the Gita. He learned about duty, righteousness, and detachment, and watched as the warriors on the battlefield embodied these principles with their every action. He observed Arjuna grappling with his doubts and fears, and saw a mirror to his own struggles. The concept of 'Nishkama Karma', or the philosophy of performing one's duty without attachment to the results, struck a chord within him. His depression, his feelings of worthlessness, were tied to his attachment to the outcomes of his actions. He realized that he needed to focus on his actions, on his duties, without the burden of their results weighing him down. Kriyansh then introduced him to 'Dhyana', the art of meditation, a practice of focusing one's mind. Yash realized that his mind was akin to a stormy sea, his thoughts like turbulent waves that tossed him around. He understood that he needed to calm his mind, to rein in his thoughts, and to achieve a state of inner peace. As Yash journeyed deeper into the teachings of the Gita, he felt a transformation within him. His fears and doubts began to recede, replaced by a newfound sense of purpose and determination. His depression started to lift, replaced by a sense of calm and tranquility. His perspective on life began to shift, his outlook becoming more positive. As the war raged on, Yash found himself changing, evolving. He was no longer the man who had once contemplated suicide, who had felt worthless and unloved. He was metamorphosing into a man who understood his duties, who knew how to focus, who had learned to control his emotions. As he stood on the battlefield of Kurukshetra, watching the warriors fight with unwavering determination, he realized that he too was a warrior. He was a warrior fighting his own battles, a warrior learning to overcome his fears and doubts, a warrior on a journey to find himself. And so, as the sun set on the battlefield of Kurukshetra, casting long shadows that danced eerily in the twilight, Yash found himself looking forward to the battles that lay ahead. He knew that the journey would be fraught with challenges and setbacks, but he also knew that he was not alone. He had Kriyansh by his side - his guide, his mentor, his friend. As he stared at the setting sun, a sense of peace enveloped him. He knew he was on the right path, that he was inching closer towards a brighter future. And for the first time in what seemed like a lifetime, he felt hopeful, he felt alive. And so, their journey into the past continued, each day unveiling new lessons, each day offering new insights. As Yash delved deeper into the teachings of the Gita, he found himself growing, evolving, metamorphosing into a better version of himself. A version that was stronger, wiser, and more resilient. And as he stood there, on the precipice of the battlefield, he realized that this was just the beginning. The beginning of a journey of self-discovery, of self-transformation, a journey that would change his life forever.

Chapter 5

The Battlefield of Life

On the second day of the war, as the sun began its ascent, painting the canvas of the sky in a palette of brilliant orange and scarlet hues, Yash found himself standing alongside Kriyansh. They were on the precipice of the battlefield, watching the two vast armies preparing for the day's battle. The air was thick with tension, anticipation, and a sense of impending doom. The battlefield, which had been a theatre of chaos and carnage the previous day, now lay eerily silent, as if holding its breath before the storm. This calm, however, was a thinly veiled illusion, a mere interlude in the symphony of war that would soon resume its brutal melody. Yet, amidst this turmoil, Yash felt an unusual sense of serenity. He was not here as a mere spectator, but as a seeker of answers. He had questions that gnawed at his peace, and he hoped to find their answers in the lessons of history that unfolded before him. Over the course of the next five days, Yash was subjected to the harsh, brutal realities of war. The war was a masterclass in the dance of life and death, a spectacle of the human capacity for both valor and malevolence. He watched as towering warriors fell, their bodies hitting the ground with a thud that echoed the impermanence of life. He saw bonds of friendship strained and tested under the weight of duty and allegiance. He saw the devastating consequences of unchecked greed and inflated ego, laying bare the destructive potential of the human psyche. Amidst the bloodshed and destruction, he also witnessed acts of unparalleled courage, self-sacrifice, and the indomitable spirit of righteousness. The first day was a showcase of Bhishma's awe-inspiring might. Bhishma, the venerable patriarch of the Kuru clan, despite his age, fought with the fervor and agility of a young warrior. His arrows, swift and precise, caused tremendous damage to the Pandavas army. However, Bhishma's unwavering loyalty to the throne, despite recognizing the Kauravas' injustice, stirred within Yash profound questions about the true essence of duty and righteousness. As he watched Bhishma, the stalwart warrior, cleave through the

Pandavas forces, his mind grappled with the complex interplay of duty, honor, and morality. Could blind allegiance, even in the face of blatant wrongdoing, be considered righteous? Or did righteousness demand the courage to question, to rebel against injustice, even if it meant going against one's sworn duty? The second day of the war was a testament to the power of unity and strategic planning. Watching the Pandavas regroup to counter Bhishma's devastating attacks, Yash realized the importance of unity in overcoming formidable challenges. The sight of the five Pandavas brothers, each unique in their skills yet fighting as a single unit, was an inspiration. It was a testament to their fraternal bond, a bond that remained unbroken in the face of adversity. It was a reminder that unity, when combined with strategy, can turn the tide of the most daunting battles. The third day of the war brought home the grim reality of war - death. Yash watched as countless warriors fell, their bodies strewn across the battlefield, their dreams and ambitions buried with them. He saw the life gradually drain out of the eyes of these warriors, their bodies going limp, their spirits departing for the heavenly abode. This stark tableau of lifeless bodies, silent testimonies to the futility of war, underscored the preciousness and fragility of life. It was a chilling reminder of the transient nature of life, a lesson in the inevitability of death. The fourth day marked the entrance of Abhimanyu, Arjuna's valiant son, into the battlefield. Abhimanyu, despite his tender age, had the heart of a lion. Trapped in the Chakravyuh, a convoluted and deadly battle formation, he refused to surrender. The Chakravyuh was an impregnable formation, a deadly maze designed to trap and kill the enemy. Its intricacies were known only to a select few. Abhimanyu, who had learnt about it while in his mother's womb, was familiar with the technique to penetrate this deadly formation but was unaware of how to exit it. It was like venturing into a labyrinth with no knowledge of the path leading out. Undeterred by this handicap, the young warrior took the challenge head-on. He breached the Chakravyuh, causing significant damage to the Kauravas army. He fought with a courage and determination that belied his age, his actions inspiring the beleaguered Pandava army. However, trapped within the deadly labyrinth of the Chakravyuh, his valiant fight ended in a tragic death. The sight of Abhimanyu's lifeless body, the young warrior who had fought with the courage of a seasoned soldier, was a stark reminder of the cost of courage and the price of duty. It was a lesson in the inevitable sacrifices that one must make in the pursuit of righteousness. The aftermath of Abhimanyu's death was a heart-wrenching scene.

Arjuna, his father, was a picture of grief. His eyes, usually calm and composed, now reflected a tempest of sorrow and rage. His hands, which had wielded the Gandiva with unwavering steadiness, now trembled with the weight of his loss. Lord Krishna, Arjuna's charioteer, and mentor, shared in his grief. But in this moment of despair, he reminded Arjuna of his duty as a warrior and the impermanence of life. He recounted the teachings of the Gita, where he had emphasized the immortality of the soul. He reminded Arjuna that the body was merely a vessel, a temporary abode for the eternal soul. The fifth day brought with it a new lesson as Dronacharya, the revered teacher of both the Pandavas and Kauravas, took command of the Kaurava army. The sight of the esteemed guru, now the enemy commander, filled Yash with a sense of irony. Dronacharya, who had once taught the Pandavas the art of warfare, was now using that very knowledge against them. Dronacharya's decision to fight against his own students, despite knowing their righteousness, led Yash to question the delicate line separating right from wrong. It forced him to ponder the duality of morality and duty, and the often-blurred line that separates the two. Each day brought with it a new lesson, a new perspective. As Yash watched the war unfold, he began to see his personal struggles mirrored in the war. He realized that his problems, much like the war, were borne out of his own doubts, fears, and insecurities. He saw his struggles reflected in the dilemmas of the warriors, their victories, and their defeats. And he understood that just like the warriors on the battlefield, he too had the power to overcome his struggles. As the last rays of the sun receded on the fifth day, Yash found himself standing on the battlefield, his mind teeming with the day's lessons. He realized that the battlefield of Kurukshetra was not just a physical battlefield but a metaphor for life. Each warrior, each battle, each victory, and each defeat held a lesson that could guide him through the battlefield of life. The battlefield was a mirror, reflecting the struggles of life, the dilemmas of choice, and the consequences of actions. As he stood there, lost in his thoughts, Kriyansh approached him. "Yash," he began, "Do you remember the verse from the Bhagavad Gita where Krishna says, 'Karmanye Vadhikaraste Ma Phaleshu Kadachana'?"

Yash nodded, recognizing the verse as one of the most quoted and interpreted ones from the Bhagavad Gita. "It means 'You have the right to perform your duties, but you are not entitled to the fruits of your actions'," Yash recollected. Kriyansh affirmed, "That's correct. But do you understand its depth, Yash? Do you comprehend its relevance to your life?"

Yash pondered upon this. He had heard and read this verse many times, but he had not fully grasped its profound meaning or its relevance to his life. "I suppose it implies that we should concentrate on our duties, on our actions, and not be overly concerned about the results," he ventured. Kriyansh nodded. "That's part of it," he conceded, "But it's not just about focusing on your duties. It's about performing your duties without attachment, without expectation. It's about acknowledging that the results of your actions are not under your control, that they are dictated by the laws of karma. It's about understanding that your worth is not defined by the results of your actions, but by the actions themselves."

As the sun set on the battlefield of Kurukshetra, Yash found himself viewing the war, his life, from a fresh perspective. He realized that he was not just an onlooker of the war, but a warrior himself. He was not merely a victim of his circumstances but an architect of his destiny. He realized that he had the power to change his life, to overcome his struggles, to find the peace and happiness he so desperately sought. As the remnants of the day faded into the night, Yash looked forward to the battles that awaited him. He knew the journey would be fraught with difficulties and challenges. But he also knew that he was ready, that he was prepared. He knew he had the strength, the courage, and the wisdom to face whatever lay ahead. And so, their journey into the past continued, each day unveiling new lessons, new insights. As Yash delved deeper into the teachings of the Gita, he felt himself growing, evolving, metamorphosing into a better version of himself. As he walked through the pages of history, he felt himself stepping closer to understanding his true self, his purpose, his destiny. He felt the burden of his doubts, his fears, his insecurities, slowly lifting. He felt a sense of peace, a sense of calm, washing over him. Each day, each lesson, was a stepping stone on his journey of self-discovery. Each day brought him closer to finding the answers he sought. And with each passing day, he felt a sense of hope, a sense of optimism, slowly replacing the despair, the hopelessness that had once consumed him. And so, as the sun set on the fifth day of the war, Yash found himself standing at the cusp of a new beginning, ready to face the battles that lay ahead. He was no longer a mere spectator, but an active participant in the theatre of life. He was no longer a victim of his circumstances, but a warrior, ready to fight his battles, ready to write his destiny. As he stood there, under the vast expanse of the sky, he felt a sense of hope, a sense of purpose, washing over him. He knew he was on the right path, and he was ready to walk it, no matter what lay ahead.

Chapter 6

The Twist of Time

A curtain of silence descended over the battlefield as the fifth day of the cataclysmic Kurukshetra war reached its end. Yash, an observer amidst the echoes of clashing swords and cries of fallen warriors, found himself immersed in a profound torrent of emotions. This journey into the past, a realm far removed from his familiar world, was as enlightening as it was disconcerting. He yearned for the familiarity of his existence, however flawed and chaotic it may have been. He missed the humdrum of his everyday life, the faces of his friends and family, the rhythm of his routines. He felt like a ship adrift in the vast ocean, yearning for the sight of familiar shores. Casting a glance at Kriyansh, his spiritual guide in this strange world, he said, "I want to go back, Kriy." His voice was thick with longing, "I want to go back to my life."

Kriyansh, who had been observing Yash quietly, turned towards him. His ancient eyes, mirrors to countless wars and the rise and fall of civilizations, reflected a deep understanding. He had seen this internal struggle before - the conflict between the comfort of the known and the wisdom of the unknown. It was a duel as old as time itself. "Yash," he responded, his voice gentle, "your life on Earth is over."

The words struck Yash like a bolt of lightning. His heart pounded in his chest as he stared at Kriyansh, disbelief etched across his face. "What do you mean?" he questioned, his voice barely a whisper against the unsettling quietude of the dusk. "Your physical body, your life as you knew it, is no more," explained Kriyansh, maintaining his serene demeanor. "But your spirit, your consciousness, is here with me. You're in a state of transition, Yash. A state of evolving."

Yash fell silent, his mind a whirlpool of thoughts and emotions. He had embarked on this journey hoping to find answers, a resolution to his misery. He had hoped to return to his old life with a newfound understanding of his struggles. But he had never imagined that he would never be able to return, that he had left it behind for good. "Why me, Kriy?" Yash voiced out his desperation. "Why did you choose me? I'm a non-believer, a man who's lost his way. Why help me?"

Kriyansh looked at Yash, his eyes brimming with compassion. "Because you were ready, Yash," he replied, his voice gentle. "Ready to learn, ready to change. Your struggles, your doubts, they were a call for help. And I answered."

"But I want magic, Kriy," Yash said, his voice choked with longing. "I want my life to change, to become better. Can't you do that?"

Kriyansh shook his head gently, "Magic, as you call it, doesn't exist, Yash," he replied. "Change comes from within, from understanding and accepting the lessons life teaches us. Change isn't something that happens overnight. It's a process, a journey that requires time, patience, and effort. It's about making choices, about taking responsibility for your actions." Then, he continued, "Take Karna, for instance. Despite being born to a charioteer, he rose to become a great warrior due to his deeds. He chose to walk the path of righteousness, to fight for what he believed in, despite the challenges and obstacles in his path. Or consider Abhimanyu, who despite his young age, showed immense courage and fought valiantly in the Chakravyuh. Their stories teach us that our circumstances don't define us, our actions do." As Yash absorbed Kriyansh's words, he felt a shift in his perspective. He realized that his journey was far from over. He had more to learn, more to understand. And as the sun set on the fifth day of the war, Yash prepared himself for the lessons the next days would bring. He felt a newfound determination filling his heart, a newfound resolve to face whatever lay ahead. In this strange world, surrounded by the vestiges of a bygone era, Yash began to contemplate the depth of the knowledge he was acquiring. The lessons from the past began to form a tapestry of wisdom, helping him understand the very fabric of his existence. He was being shown a mirror to his life, reflecting not only his triumphs but also his failures. He was being taught the true essence of life – that it was not a bed of roses, but a path filled with thorns and obstacles. A path that required courage, determination, and above all, faith to navigate. His journey had started with a search for answers. Answers to his struggles, his doubts, his fears. But as he delved deeper, he realized that the answers he sought were not external. They were within him, waiting to be discovered. The stories of Karna, Abhimanyu, and other warriors were not just stories. They were life lessons, guiding lights illuminating his path. The story of Karna taught him that one's birth does not define one's life. It is one's actions, one's deeds that carve one's destiny. Karna, despite being born in a low caste, rose to become one of the greatest warriors of his time. His story was a testament to the fact that one can rise above their circumstances if they have the courage to fight, the determination to succeed. Then there was Abhimanyu, the young prince who fought valiantly in the Chakravyuh despite knowing that he wouldn't come out alive. His story taught Yash the value of courage, the importance of standing up for what one believes in, even if it means walking into the jaws of death. As Yash reflected on these lessons, he felt a sense of enlightenment washing over him. He began to see his life in a new light. His struggles no longer seemed insurmountable. His doubts, his fears began to fade away, replaced by a newfound sense of courage, a newfound determination. As the dusk gave way to the night, Yash found himself standing at the precipice of a new beginning. He was ready to take the leap, to dive into the unknown. He was ready to explore the depths of his consciousness, to unearth the wisdom hidden within. He was ready to learn, to grow, to evolve. And with that, he looked at Kriyansh, a sense of gratitude filling his heart. "Thank you, Kriy," he said, his voice filled with emotion. "For everything." Kriyansh turned to look at him, a smile playing on his lips. "The journey has just begun, Yash," he said. "There's a lot more to learn, a lot more to explore. Are you ready?"

Yash nodded, a determined look in his eyes. "I am," he said. And with that, they both turned to look at the horizon, the setting sun casting long shadows on the battlefield. It was the end of a day, the end of a chapter. But it was also the beginning of a new journey, a journey into the depths of wisdom, a journey into the heart of the self. As the last rays of the setting sun disappeared beyond the horizon, Yash and Kriyansh stood there, side by side, ready to embark on the next chapter of their journey. A journey that would change Yash's life, a journey that would help him find the answers he was seeking, a journey that would lead him to the truth. As the stars began to twinkle in the night sky, Yash looked at Kriyansh, a sense of anticipation filling his heart. He was ready to delve deeper into the mysteries of life, ready to unravel the secrets of the universe, ready to explore the depths of his consciousness. And with that thought, he looked at the star-studded sky, a sense of peace washing over him. He was on a journey, a journey of self-discovery, a journey of enlightenment. And he was ready to embrace whatever lay ahead, ready to face the challenges, ready to learn the lessons. Under the starlit sky, Yash and Kriyansh stood there, ready to embark on the next chapter of their journey.

A journey into the heart of the self, a journey into the depths of wisdom, a journey that would change their lives forever. As the night descended, they both looked at the sky, the stars twinkling like tiny diamonds in the velvet darkness. It was a sight that was both beautiful and humbling, a reminder of the vastness of the universe, of the infiniteness of life. As they stood there, under the vast expanse of the starlit sky, they both knew that they were on the right path. They were on a journey, a journey of discovery, a journey of enlightenment. And they were ready. Ready to delve deeper into the mysteries of life, ready to unravel the secrets of the universe, ready to explore the depths of their consciousness. And with that thought, Yash and Kriyansh stood there, under the starlit sky, ready to embark on the next chapter of their journey. A journey that would take them deeper into the mysteries of life, a journey that would lead them to the truth, a journey that would change their lives forever. And so, under the boundless expanse of the night sky, as the first chapter of their incredible journey came to an end, Yash and Kriyansh prepared themselves for the many revelations, trials, and transformations that lay ahead. They were ready. Ready to delve deeper, ready to learn, ready to evolve

Chapter 7

The Dream and the Reality

The fifth day of the epic war had come to an end, and the battlefield of Kurukshetra was quiet under the starlit sky. As the tranquility of the night took hold, Yash felt a strange sense of calm seeping into him. His mind, which had been a whirlwind of thoughts and emotions since the start of this journey, was finally quiet. His body, weary from the intensity of the experiences and lessons, yearned for rest. As he lay down on the cold ground, sleep took him into its comforting embrace. His slumber was deep, but not dreamless. He found himself in the familiar setting of his own time and place. He was back in his city, the city of towering buildings and bustling streets, of honking cars and chattering people. He found himself seated in the comforting ambience of his favourite café, a place where he had spent countless hours laughing and chatting with his friends. Across the table sat Neha and Ashish, their faces bright and cheerful as they engaged in a light-hearted banter. These were his friends, his confidantes, the ones with whom he shared the minutest details of his life. As the dream progressed, he found himself sharing his extraordinary experiences of being in the era of Mahabharata and having met Lord Krishna. The reaction of his friends, however, was not what he had expected. Instead of awe and curiosity, there was disbelief and laughter. His profound experiences and the wisdom he had gained were dismissed as a fantastical story spun by his overactive imagination. As he insisted on the truth of his experiences, their laughter only grew louder. His frustration built up, turning into a gnawing feeling of being misunderstood and ridiculed. He wanted to prove to them that he had indeed changed, that the wisdom he had gained was real and transformative. To demonstrate this transformation, he tried to apply the teachings of Krishna to his current life situations in the dream. He tried to practice patience with his overbearing boss, Naksh Sharma, and he attempted to console Neha and Ashish, who were on the verge of a bitter divorce. He even attempted to reconcile with his parents, whose perpetual disappointment in him had always been a thorn in his heart. However, every scenario in which he tried to apply his new-found wisdom resulted in further chaos. His well-intentioned efforts were either misunderstood or dismissed, leading to more discord in his relationships. His professional life suffered, and his attempts at reconciliation were met with resistance. His dream, which had started as a pleasant journey to his old life, turned into a nightmare. He woke up abruptly, his heart pounding, and found himself back on the battlefield. The dream had been so vivid that it took him a few moments to register his surroundings. As the first rays of the morning sun touched the ground, he sought Kriyansh. He narrated his dream, his voice shaking as he recounted the experiences. Kriyansh listened quietly, his face a mask of calmness. When Yash finished, Kriyansh spoke. His voice was soft, but it held a firmness that demanded attention. "Yash," he began, "your dream reflects your fears and apprehensions. It's showing you the consequences of half-understood knowledge applied without discernment." Kriyansh's words were like a splash of cold water, snapping Yash out of his confusion. He realized his mistake: in his eagerness to prove himself, he had tried to apply the teachings without fully understanding them. He had focused on the superficial aspect of the teachings, overlooking their deeper, more profound meaning. With the dawn of the sixth day, Yash found himself in contemplation. The battlefield, which had been a place of carnage and chaos, now felt like a sanctuary of wisdom. He realized that this journey was not just about learning from Krishna but also about understanding the essence of these teachings and applying them wisely. The rest of the day was spent in intense learning and introspection. Each lesson from Kriyansh was like a piece of a puzzle, slowly helping Yash form a clearer picture of life and his role in it. As the sun began to set, he couldn't help but marvel at the transformation he was undergoing. The battlefield, with all its grim realities, was becoming a place of growth and self-realization. The sight of the setting sun was a reminder of the transient nature of life. It was a spectacle of hope, promising a new day and new opportunities to learn and grow. As night descended, Yash found himself looking forward to the lessons the next day would bring. His dream had been a wake-up call, and he was now more determined than ever to fully grasp the wisdom of the teachings. With a renewed sense of purpose, Yash welcomed the seventh day of the war. He realized that each day was an opportunity for him to learn and grow, to understand life a little better. As he moved forward on his journey, he felt a profound sense of gratitude for Kriyansh, who was not just his guide but also his mentor and friend. His journey in the past was shaping his present and future, and he was eager to see where it would lead him.

The night after his unsettling dream, Yash found solace in the gentle hum of the campfires that dotted the vast plains of Kurukshetra. The distant constellations seemed to whisper age-old secrets. With each passing moment, he felt the weight of his dream, the stinging laughter of disbelief, and the chaos that ensued when he applied his learnings haphazardly. He remembered the precise expressions on Neha and Ashish's faces. Neha, with her long, wavy hair cascading down her shoulders, had an amused glint in her eyes, her lips curled in a playful smirk. Ashish, on the other hand, had thrown his head back in laughter, his glasses almost slipping off. The café, which once resonated with shared memories and laughter, felt cold and distant. The aroma of freshly brewed coffee, which once felt comforting, now seemed to mock his outlandish tales. Yet, it wasn't just the laughter that haunted Yash. It was also the vividness of the dream—how real everything felt. The texture of the café's wooden table, the ambient music playing softly in the background, the scent of Neha's familiar perfume, and the gravity in Ashish's voice when he later confided about his marital troubles.

In the dream, he had visited Neha and Ashish's home—a modern apartment with sleek furniture and panoramic views of the city. The walls, which were once adorned with their travel memories and candid laughter, were now stained with the scars of heated arguments. He could hear the hushed whispers of their neighbors, speculating the reasons for their sudden discord. As Yash tried to mediate between them, he felt the vast chasm that had grown between the couple. He remembered Ashish's words, "Yash, it's easy for you to preach about patience and understanding when you're just a visitor in our lives. You don't understand the depths of our issues." Neha, tears streaming down her face, had added, "Maybe if you focused on your own life, you'd see the flaws in your wisdom."

The dream shifted, and Yash found himself in his office, a modern workspace with glass cabins and open desks. He tried to apply the principles of dharma and righteousness in his dealings, standing up against the unethical practices of his boss, Naksh Sharma. But instead of appreciation, he was met with ridicule. "This isn't some ancient scripture, Yash. This is the real world," Naksh had sneered, his eyes cold and dismissive. As Yash sat there, under the vast canopy of stars, he realized the profoundness of Kriyansh's teachings about the perils of half-baked knowledge. The dream had shown him a mirror, reflecting the consequences of superficial understanding. True wisdom wasn't just about knowing; it was about understanding and applying judiciously. With a heavy heart, Yash approached Kriyansh's tent. The sage, sensing his arrival, invited him in. The interior of the tent was simple, with a dimly lit lamp casting shadows on the canvas walls. Yet, there was an air of serenity.

Yash narrated the events of his dream, the pain evident in his voice. As he spoke, Kriyansh's gaze never wavered, absorbing every word, every emotion. Once Yash finished, Kriyansh spoke, "Dreams are a reflection of our subconscious, a manifestation of our deepest fears and desires. Your dream has shown you the repercussions of premature application of knowledge." He continued, "Life isn't a race, Yash. It's a journey. And on this journey, understanding is as crucial as knowing. Just as a doctor wouldn't prescribe medicine without diagnosing the ailment, you shouldn't apply teachings without understanding the nuances." They talked deep into the night, with Kriyansh elaborating on various facets of life. They discussed the importance of timing, the essence of relationships, and the balance between learning and application. By the time the first light of dawn painted the horizon, Yash felt transformed. He realized he was at the cusp of a new understanding, a deeper connection with the teachings.

The battlefield, which was about to witness another day of intense warfare, was also a crucible of learning for Yash. With Kriyansh by his side, he was ready to dive deeper, to truly understand the profound wisdom that the Mahabharata offered. The journey of self-discovery was far from over, but Yash was no longer the same man who had started it. He was evolving, transforming, and he was eager to see where this path would lead him next.

Top of Form

Chapter 8

The Midst of War

As dawn broke on the sixth day, Yash was awakened by the blaring trumpets of war. The air, heavy with the stench of blood and fear, was filled with the cacophony of clashing weapons, the screams of pain from fallen warriors, and the ground-shaking roars of war elephants. The earth beneath his feet, once a lush green field, was now stained a grim red, littered with the lifeless bodies of countless soldiers. Their dreams, hopes, and ambitions lay buried alongside them, a silent testament to the cruel hand of war. As Yash walked across the battlefield, the sight of Bhima on the sixth day was etched into his memory. Bhima, one of the mighty Pandava brothers, was a sight to behold. His towering figure loomed over the battlefield; his rage palpable in the air around him. He cut through the Kaurava army with the ferocity of a tempest, his mace swinging like a destructive whirlwind. The very ground seemed to tremble under the might of his blows. The sight of Bhima's wrath was a vivid demonstration of the destructive power of uncontrolled anger. Yash realized that like Bhima's uncontrolled rage, his own unchecked anger and frustration could lead to destructive consequences. The seventh day brought with it new lessons in the form of Dronacharya, the formidable commander of the Kaurava army. A master strategist and an unparalleled warrior, Dronacharya used his divine Astras (weapons) to wreak havoc on the Pandava army. He was a force to be reckoned with, his power evident in every swift movement, every calculated attack. But it was the unchecked use of his power that led to massive destruction, a harsh reminder of the dire consequences of power devoid of responsibility and morality. Watching Dronacharya, Yash understood that power, when not balanced with responsibility and morality, could lead to destruction and chaos. This was a lesson he could apply to his present life, where he had often let his position and power cloud his judgment. The eighth day of the war introduced Yash to the power of strategy and teamwork. Despite being outnumbered and outpowered, the Pandava brothers worked in perfect harmony, countering Dronacharya's relentless attacks. Their unity and strategic planning stood as a formidable wall against the might of the Kaurava army. It was a testament to the strength that lies in unity and strategic planning. This realization hit Yash hard, making him understand the importance of teamwork and strategic planning in overcoming challenges, something he had often overlooked in his life. However, the ninth day of the war unfolded a harsh reality - the fall of Bhishma Pitamah. Bhishma, the grand old warrior, invincible due to his boon of choosing the time of his death, was a symbol of valor and righteousness. His body lay on a bed of arrows, a sight that sent a wave of shock and sorrow across the battlefield. The warrior, who had fought for the wrong side despite knowing the truth, lay defeated, his life seeping away slowly. This image was etched into Yash's mind, a stark reminder of the importance of standing up for what is right, even when it's difficult. With each passing day, the war at Kurukshetra was transforming Yash's perspective towards life. He had started to view his own struggles and problems in a new light. He understood that his problems, much like the war, were a result of his own actions and choices. And just like the warriors on the battlefield, he too had the power to overcome them. As the ninth day of the war came to an end, Yash found himself looking forward to the lessons the next days would bring. His heart was filled with a sense of anticipation, a thirst to unravel the knowledge that lay ahead. He was eager to learn, to grow, to become a better version of himself. Little did he know that the most important lesson was yet to come. With every passing day, the war was unravelling new facets of life and wisdom before Yash. The lessons were harsh, the realities bitter, but the knowledge invaluable. He was slowly beginning to understand the profound wisdom hidden in the epic war, the wisdom that was as relevant in the present day as it was thousands of years ago. With every sunrise, he was learning to look beyond the visible, to see the unseen, to understand the unspoken. As the tenth day dawned, Yash found himself standing on the precipice of a new understanding, a new realization. He was ready to dive deeper into the sea of wisdom, to navigate the turbulent waves of change. He was ready to embrace the journey, with all its trials and tribulations, its joys, and sorrows. The war at Kurukshetra was more than a historical event for Yash. It was a mirror, reflecting his own life, his own struggles. It was a teacher, imparting invaluable lessons. It was a journey, leading him towards self-discovery and enlightenment. And as he stood there, on the tenth day, looking at the rising sun, Yash knew that he was ready. Ready to face the day, ready to learn, ready to change. For he now understood that change is not something that happens overnight. It is a process, a journey that requires patience, understanding, and courage. And he was ready to embark on this journey, ready to navigate the path that lay ahead. For Yash, the war at Kurukshetra was no longer a distant event in the past. It was a part of his present, a part of his journey. It was a guide, leading him towards the path of wisdom, the path of enlightenment. It was a beacon of light, illuminating the path ahead, guiding him through the darkness of ignorance. As he stood there, on the tenth day of the war, Yash felt a sense of calmness envelop him. He was no longer the same person who had walked onto the battlefield on the first day. He had grown, he had learned, he had changed. He had begun to understand the true essence of life, the true meaning of his existence. The war at Kurukshetra was a turning point in Yash's life. It was a catalyst, triggering a transformation within him. And as he stood there, on the tenth day, he knew that he was ready. Ready to face the challenges that lay ahead, ready to learn from his mistakes, ready to change. And so, with a renewed sense of purpose, Yash stepped into the tenth day of the war, his heart filled with determination, his mind open to learning. He knew that the journey ahead was long and difficult, but he was ready to face it, to overcome it. For he now understood that every challenge is an opportunity to learn, every obstacle a stepping stone towards growth. With every passing day, Yash was becoming more attuned to the wisdom of the epic war. He was learning to see beyond the apparent chaos and destruction, to understand the profound lessons hidden within it. He was beginning to realize that the war was not just a historical event, but a timeless guide to life and wisdom. As Yash delved deeper into the teachings of the war, he began to see a reflection of his own life, his own struggles. He realized that like the warriors on the battlefield, he too was fighting his own battles, battling his own demons. And just like the warriors, he too had the power to overcome them, to emerge victorious. With each passing day, Yash was growing, evolving, transforming. He was shedding his old self, embracing a new understanding, a new perspective. He was learning to navigate the complexities of life, to face the challenges with courage and resilience. As he stood on the precipice of a new day, Yash knew that he was ready. Ready to face the challenges that lay ahead, ready to learn from the wisdom of the war, ready to evolve. For he now understood that life is not a battlefield, but a journey. A journey of self-discovery, a journey of growth, a journey of enlightenment. And with this newfound understanding, Yash stepped into the tenth day of the war, his heart filled with courage, his mind open to learning. He was ready to face the day, ready to embrace the lessons, ready to grow. With the dawn of the tenth day, Yash found himself standing at the threshold of a new understanding, a new realization. He was ready to delve deeper into the sea of wisdom, to unravel the profound lessons hidden within the war. He was ready to embark on a journey of self-discovery, a journey of enlightenment. As he stood there, on the threshold of a new day, Yash felt a sense of calm envelop him. And so, with a renewed sense of purpose, Yash stepped into the tenth day of the war. He was ready to face the challenges that lay ahead, ready to learn from the wisdom of the war, ready to evolve. He knew that the journey ahead was long and difficult, but he was ready to face it, ready to overcome it. With every passing day, Yash was growing, evolving, transforming. He knew that the journey ahead was not only about surviving the war but also about understanding its profound teachings. The tenth day brought with it an air of uncertainty. Even as the sun rose, casting long shadows on the battlefield, Yash could feel a sense of unease. But amidst the chaos and fear, Yash found a sense of purpose. He was not just a spectator to the war anymore; he was a participant, learning and growing with each passing day. The battlefield had become his classroom, the warriors his teachers, the war his lesson. As the day progressed, Yash found himself drawn to the various strategies employed by the warriors. He watched as the Pandavas and Kauravas, each with their unique strengths and weaknesses, used various tactics to gain an advantage. He saw the importance of adaptability, of changing strategies as the situation demanded, and the futility of sticking to rigid plans. It was a lesson in flexibility and adaptability, one that Yash knew he could apply in his life. While the war raged on, Yash also observed the leadership qualities displayed by the leaders of both armies. He saw how the leaders motivated their soldiers, how they strategized and planned, how they dealt with setbacks, and how they led by example. Yash realized that leadership was not about power and authority but about inspiring and guiding others. As the tenth day ended, Yash found himself reflecting on the lessons of the day. He realized that the teachings of the battlefield were not limited to warfare but applied to life as well. Whether it was the importance of adaptability, the essence of good leadership, or the value of teamwork, each lesson had a deeper, more profound meaning. As he lay on the cold, hard ground, staring at the star-studded sky, Yash felt a sense of calm wash over him. The sounds of the battlefield had faded into a distant hum, and all he could hear was the quiet whisper of the wind. In the silence of the night, Yash found clarity. He knew that the lessons he had learned were not just for the battlefield but for life as well. He understood that just like the warriors, he too was on a journey, a journey of self-discovery, growth, and enlightenment. With each passing day, Yash was evolving. He was not the same person who had entered the battlefield on the first day. The war had changed him, shaped him, made him stronger. He was growing, not just in age but in wisdom and understanding. And as he drifted into sleep, Yash knew that he was ready for the journey ahead. For he was not just a spectator to the war, but a participant. And he was ready to face whatever the next day brought with courage, resilience, and an open mind. And so, with a heart full of hope and a mind open to learning, Yash awaited the dawn of a new day. A day that would bring new challenges, new lessons, and new opportunities for growth. For Yash, the war was not just a battle between two factions; it was a journey, a journey towards self-discovery, growth, and enlightenment. And he was ready to embark on this journey, ready to learn, ready to grow, and ready to change. As the tenth day of the war ended, Yash found himself at the cusp of a new understanding. He had seen the war, not just as a battle between good and evil, but as a mirror reflecting his own life, his own struggles. He had seen the warriors, not just as figures from a forgotten era, but as guides, leading him on his journey of self-discovery. He had seen the battlefield, not just as a land of death and destruction, but as a classroom, teaching him invaluable lessons about life. As he looked forward to the dawn of a new day, Yash knew that he was ready. For Yash, the war at Kurukshetra was a turning point in his life.

The tenth night on the battlefield was eerily quiet compared to the days filled with tumultuous battles. The soft glow of the moonlight illuminated the vast expanse, revealing the scars left behind by the day's events. Yash sat in quiet contemplation, the lessons of the day echoing in his mind. The war was not just a historical event for him but a tapestry of life lessons woven intricately. Each day, each warrior, each strategy held a lesson, a message, a deeper meaning. Late into the night, Yash was approached by a figure. It was Arjuna, the chief protagonist of the Pandavas. His eyes, usually sharp and focused, now looked weary, bearing the weight of the choices he made and the lives lost due to them. Sitting beside Yash, Arjuna began recounting tales from his childhood, lessons he learned, and the guidance he received from Krishna.

The conversation shifted to the burdens they both felt, albeit in different eras and circumstances. Arjuna spoke of the weight of responsibilities, the conflict of duty over emotions, and the constant battle within oneself. Yash found solace in Arjuna's words, realizing that the struggles of the human heart remained consistent over time. The specifics might change, but the essence of human conflicts, dilemmas, and moral quandaries remained similar.

Arjuna shared a valuable piece of wisdom, "In life, Yash, battles are not always fought on fields with weapons. Some are fought within, and those are often the toughest. The decisions we make, the paths we choose, they shape our destiny. And amidst all this, it's essential to find our own 'dharma', our true purpose." As the conversation deepened, Yash shared his experiences, the mistakes he made, the regrets he held. Arjuna, in return, offered insights, drawing parallels from his own life, making Yash realize the cyclical nature of life's challenges. As the first light of dawn began to break, the two men, from different eras, found common ground. They realized that while the settings, times, and challenges differed, the essence of the human journey remained unchanged. It was about introspection, understanding one's purpose, making choices, and living with their consequences.

Arjuna, sensing the day's battle approaching, offered Yash a quiver of arrows. "These are not ordinary arrows," he said, "each one symbolizes a lesson, a principle, a value. Use them wisely in your battles, both external and internal." Accepting the quiver, Yash felt a surge of energy. The weight of the arrows reminded him of the weight of the lessons and the responsibilities they carried. The tenth day, while physically exhausting, had been mentally and spiritually enlightening.

The war, with its raw display of human emotions, had become a profound learning experience for Yash. It was teaching him about resilience, about morality, about the grey areas in life's decisions, and the significance of introspection and self-awareness. As the battle cries began signaling the start of another day, Yash, with the quiver on his back, felt better equipped to face his challenges, both in the war and in life. The war at Kurukshetra, while a grim reminder of the destruction humans could cause, was also a beacon of hope and wisdom for him. He had come to understand that life's true battles were not always fought on battlegrounds but within oneself. And with the right guidance, introspection, and lessons, one could navigate these challenges with grace and wisdom. The journey was long, and the path arduous, but with the lessons from Kurukshetra embedded in his heart, Yash was ready to continue his quest for understanding, growth, and enlightenment.

Chapter 9

The Unseen Battle

The tenth day of the war arrived with an air of anticipation. Lord Krishna, serving as Arjuna's charioteer, was about to recite the wisdom-filled verses of the Bhagavad Gita, providing Arjuna with the guidance to navigate his doubts and fears. Yet, Yash was unaware of this divine discourse. His guide, Kriyansh, had vanished without a trace. The absence of Kriyansh left Yash alone, surrounded by the clamor of the battlefield. Yet, he was not completely alone; he was in the company of the warriors. He could feel the weight of their Armor, the sharpness of their weapons, the determination in their hearts. Every beating heart around him echoed with the same rhythm: the rhythm of war. Yash decided to approach the warriors of the Kaurava army, attempting to understand their reasons for fighting in the war. His first encounter was with Duryodhana, the ambitious prince leading the

Kaurava army. Duryodhana's eyes glinted with a thirst for power, his words echoed with an insatiable desire for the throne. As Yash listened to Duryodhana, he observed the prince's arrogance, the audacity of his entitlement. Yash's interactions didn't stop with Duryodhana. He sought out Dushasana, Duryodhana's loyal brother, and Karna, the friend of Duryodhana and a formidable warrior. From Dushasana, he learned about loyalty that bordered on blindness, loyalty that was unyielding and uncompromising. Karna, on the other hand, shared tales of gratitude and struggle, his life a saga of trials and tribulations. Through these interactions, Yash delved deeper into the intricacies of the war. He realized that the war was not just about the throne; it was a battle of ideologies, a test of dharma, a play of karma. The thirteenth day of the war concluded, leaving Yash longing for Kriyansh's guidance. Alone on the battlefield, he called out for Kriyansh, but his calls echoed in the silence of the night. Kriyansh was nowhere to be found. As the fourteenth day approached, Yash took a moment to introspect. The words of the warriors resonated within him, their motivations and justifications giving him a deeper understanding of the war. This was not just a war for a throne; it was a war of identities, of ideologies, of dharma and adharma. Despite the absence of

Kriyansh, Yash found a strange sense of calm enveloping him. He was not alone; he had the wisdom of the warriors and the lessons from the war. He was a part of this cosmic play, an observer, and a participant. Each day brought a new lesson, a new understanding. Each warrior had a story to tell, a lesson to teach. As the war progressed, Yash found himself evolving, learning, growing. He was not just observing the war; he was experiencing it. He was living it. With each passing day, Yash's anticipation grew. He was eager to learn the remaining lessons, eager to witness the unfolding of the divine plan. As he stood on the battlefield, amidst the warriors, under the vast sky, he felt a sense of connection. He felt a connection with the warriors, with the battlefield, with the war. As the sun rose, casting long shadows on the battlefield, Yash felt a renewed sense of determination. He was ready to face the upcoming days, ready to learn the remaining lessons, ready to witness the unfolding of the divine plan. Yash realized that he was not just a spectator in this cosmic play; he was a participant. He was not just observing the war; he was living it. Every sight, every sound, every smell, every feeling was a part of him, a part of his journey. As the sun rose higher, illuminating the battlefield, Yash felt a sense of anticipation. He was ready for the upcoming events, ready to embrace the lessons they would bring, ready to witness the divine plan unfold. With Kriyansh's wisdom in his heart, the lessons of the war in his mind, and the anticipation of the upcoming events in his soul, Yash was ready. As he looked out onto the battlefield, his heart filled with courage, his mind filled with wisdom, Yash knew that he was ready. With this newfound wisdom, Yash found a sense of calm. He realized that he was a part of something bigger, a part of a cosmic plan, a part of a divine play. With this realization, Yash found a sense of peace. As he stood there, on the battlefield, under the bright sun, Yash felt a sense of resolution. He was resolved to face the challenges, to learn from them, to grow. He was ready to witness the divine play, to be a part of the cosmic plan, to fulfil his destiny. As the sun cast long shadows on the battlefield, Yash felt a renewed sense of determination. He was ready to face the upcoming days, ready to embrace the lessons they would bring, ready to witness the unfolding of the divine plan. As he stood there, on the battlefield, under the bright sun, Yash felt a sense of connection. He felt a connection with the universe, with the divine, with himself. As the sun rose higher, Yash felt a sense of anticipation. He was eager to witness the upcoming events, eager to learn the remaining lessons, eager to understand the ultimate truth. As he stood there, under the bright sun, Yash felt a sense of resolution. He was resolved to face the challenges, resolved to embrace the lessons, resolved to fulfil his destiny. As he looked out onto the battlefield, his eyes filled with determination, his heart filled with courage, his soul filled with wisdom, Yash knew that he was ready. Each day on the battlefield brought a new lesson, a new understanding, a new perspective. Each conversation with the warriors, each observation of the war, each introspection brought him closer to the truth. As the sun set on the thirteenth day, Yash stood on the battlefield, ready for the days to come. He knew that the upcoming days would be challenging, but he was prepared. He was ready to face the challenges, to learn from them, to grow. With each passing day, Yash grew stronger, wiser. He was not just a spectator; he was a participant. He was a part of the cosmic play, a part of the divine plan. As the sun set, casting long shadows on the battlefield, Yash felt a sense of peace. He knew that he was not alone; he had the wisdom of the warriors, the lessons of the war, the guidance of Kriyansh. As the night descended, Yash sat alone on the battlefield, under the starlit sky. The battlefield was silent, save for the occasional cries of the wounded and the howling wind. Yash was alone, but he was at peace. He was ready for the upcoming days, ready for the challenges they would bring, ready to witness the unfolding of the divine plan. As he sat there, under the stars, Yash felt a sense of connection. He was a part of the cosmic plan, a part of the divine play, a part of the war. As the night deepened, Yash found himself lost in thought. He thought about the warriors, about their stories, their struggles, their motivations. He thought about the war, about its complexities, its intricacies. He thought about the lessons he had learned; about the wisdom he had gained. As he sat there, under the stars, Yash felt a sense of anticipation. As he sat there, under the stars, Yash felt a sense of resolution. As the night turned into dawn, Yash found himself filled with a renewed sense of determination. As the first rays of the sun illuminated the battlefield, Yash stood up, ready to face the new day. As he stood there, under the rising sun, Yash felt a sense of resolution. The absence of Kriyansh was a palpable void, a missing piece in the grand puzzle of the war. Yash felt his absence deeply, like a lost child in an unfamiliar city. The guidance and wisdom Kriyansh had provided were now replaced with a silence that echoed loudly in Yash's mind. He felt an overwhelming sense of being adrift, a small boat tossed in the tempestuous sea of the Kurukshetra war. Yash started his search for Kriyansh amidst the pandemonium of the war. His eyes darted across the battlefield, seeking the familiar figure of his mentor. His gaze swept over the sea of warriors, their faces masked with determination and fear, their bodies armored and ready for battle. He scanned the horizon, his heart pounding in his chest, his mind filled with worry. He called out to Kriyansh, his voice barely audible over the clamor of the war. His calls echoed back unanswered, swallowed by the tumultuous roar of the battlefield. The silence that followed each call was deafening, a stark contrast to the resonating chaos of the war. Each unanswered call added to Yash's growing unease, his worry transforming into a gnawing fear. As the hours passed, Yash's search grew more frantic. He moved among the warriors; his presence barely noticed in the chaos of the war. His calls for Kriyansh grew louder, more desperate, his voice hoarse from the effort. Yet, his mentor was nowhere to be found. Yash's mind was a whirlpool of thoughts, each more worrisome than the last. Had something happened to Kriyansh? Was he in trouble? Or had he left Yash alone on purpose? The questions echoed in Yash's mind; their answers elusive. The realization of his solitude hit Yash like a wave, filling him with a sense of despair. He felt lost, like a leaf adrift on a stormy sea. He was a stranger in this world, a silent observer caught in the currents of time. Without Kriyansh, he was just a man lost in a war he barely understood. As the day turned into night, Yash's hope of finding Kriyansh dwindled. He felt a growing sense of dread, a fear of the unknown. He was alone, truly alone, amidst a sea of warriors, amidst a war of epic proportions. It was a feeling that chilled him to his core. Yet, despite his growing fear, Yash felt a surge of determination. He was not going to give up, not going to succumb to despair. He had a mission, a purpose. He was here to learn, to grow, to evolve. And he was not going to let his mentor's absence deter him from his path. With this newfound resolve, Yash continued his search for Kriyansh, his calls piercing the cacophony of the war. He moved among the warriors, his gaze sharp, his spirit unwavering. He was alone, but he was not defeated. He was lost, but he was not aimless. As the night deepened, Yash found himself standing under the starlit sky, his eyes fixed on the vast expanse of the cosmos. He felt small, insignificant in the grand scheme of things. Yet, he also felt a sense of connection, a sense of being a part of something greater. He was a part of the cosmic plan, a part of the divine play. He was a participant in the war, a student of life. He was alone, but he was not lonely. He was a part of the universe, and the universe was a part of him. And so, under the starlit sky, amidst the chaos of the war, Yash stood alone, his heart filled with resolve, his spirit filled with determination. He was ready to continue his search for Kriyansh, ready to find his own path, ready to carve his own destiny. And as the first rays of dawn painted the sky in hues of gold and crimson, Yash found himself standing alone on the battlefield, his heart filled with hope, his spirit filled with determination. He was ready to face the new day, ready to continue his search for Kriyansh, ready to face whatever lay ahead. As Yash's eyes scanned the vast expanse of warriors, a figure caught his attention. It was Nakul, one of the Pandava brothers, known for his prowess in warfare and his unmatched agility on the battlefield. Beside him stood Sahdev, his twin, an equally talented warrior, but also known for his vast knowledge of medicinal herbs. Approaching them, Yash inquired about Kriyansh, but they were equally unaware of his whereabouts. Sahdev, with a calm demeanor, remarked, "Every warrior here has a purpose, a role to play, and lessons to impart. Perhaps, Kriyansh's absence is a part of your journey, Yash."

Nakul, hearing Sahdev's words, added, "In war and life, we often seek guidance externally. But there are times when we must rely on our inner wisdom." Feeling a connection with the twins, Yash shared his experiences so far, speaking of his interactions with Duryodhana, Dushasana, and Karna. Sahdev, with a reflective look, responded, "You see, Yash, while each warrior has their motivation, the essence of this war is the same for everyone. It's a battle between Dharma and Adharma." Nakul chimed in, "Sometimes the lines between right and wrong blur, making choices difficult. That's where the heart's compass and one's conscience guide the way." While their conversation flowed, a Kaurava warrior named Vikarna approached them. Known for his moral compass, Vikarna was one of the few Kauravas who questioned the public humiliation of Draupadi. He greeted Yash and the twins and added, "Often, battles are not just fought on battlefields. Inner conflicts can be more challenging than the fiercest of external wars." The three warriors and Yash sat amidst the chaos, deeply engrossed in their philosophical exchange. Their conversation touched upon loyalty, righteousness, destiny, and the importance of self-reflection.

Vikarna, with a heavy heart, confessed, "Being a Kaurava, I often grapple with my loyalties. My love for my brothers sometimes clouds my judgment, but deep down, I know where righteousness lies." Nakul, placing a reassuring hand on Vikarna's shoulder, responded, "This war is a testament to the fact that the paths of righteousness are not always straightforward. They twist and turn, challenging our beliefs and testing our resolves."

As dawn approached, Yash felt a renewed sense of purpose. The wisdom he had gained from his conversation with Nakul, Sahdev, and Vikarna was invaluable. While he missed Kriyansh's presence, he started to understand that perhaps this journey was also about forging connections, understanding varied perspectives, and finding wisdom in unexpected places. With the break of day, the war resumed with its might and fury. But Yash, even amidst the raging battle, felt a different kind of strength – one that came from understanding, introspection, and the wisdom shared by those around him. He continued his quest to find Kriyansh but with a calmer heart and a more profound understanding of his journey in this epic war. He realized that while the physical battle raged around him, an equally significant war was being fought within – a battle to understand oneself, one's purpose, and the essence of life.

The morning sun cast a golden hue on the battlefield, and amidst the tumultuous uproar, Yash sought out other warriors from the Kaurava side, hoping to understand more dimensions of the war and, perhaps, gather clues about Kriyansh. His next encounter was with Shakuni, the master strategist behind many of the Kauravas's plots and schemes. Shakuni, with his sharp eyes and cunning mind, was engrossed in a game of dice, a symbol of his manipulative nature.

"Ah! The observer of the war," Shakuni remarked with a sly grin, noticing Yash's approach. "What brings you to my camp amidst this chaos?" Curious and slightly wary, Yash replied, "I seek to understand, Maharaj, the motivations and thoughts of those who play pivotal roles in this epic tale." Chuckling, Shakuni responded, "Life itself is a game of dice, young one. Sometimes we control the roll, and sometimes we are at its mercy. But tell me, what do you wish to understand?" Yash, gathering his thoughts, said, "Your strategies, your plots, they've been central to many events leading up to this war. Why do you play these games?"

Shakuni, leaning in closer, whispered, "Power, control, and a bit of revenge. I play for my family's honor, for the perceived wrongs done to us. The dice, they're just a means to an end." The conversation was interrupted by the approach of Dronacharya, the revered teacher and now commander of the Kaurava forces. His presence was commanding, yet his eyes betrayed a hint of sadness.

Acknowledging Yash, Drona asked, "Have you found the wisdom you seek on this battlefield?"

Yash, showing his respect, replied, "Every warrior, every moment, holds a lesson, Acharya. From you, I wish to understand the weight of duty against personal beliefs."

Dronacharya sighed deeply, "I am bound by my dharma, my duty to the throne, and my students. But it pains me to see my beloved disciples on opposite sides. My heart aches when I must strategize against Arjuna, the one I've taught everything."

Shakuni smirked, "Yet, you do it. For loyalty? For duty?"

Drona, with a stern look, responded, "Loyalty, yes, but more than that, it's the complexity of dharma. It's not always black and white. Sometimes, duty demands actions that the heart revolts against."

Yash, absorbing the profoundness of the conversation, remarked, "It seems that every warrior here, regardless of the side they're on, grapples with inner conflicts."

Shakuni laughed, "Welcome to the great Kurukshetra, young observer. Where battles are fought as much within the soul as on the ground."

As the day wore on, Yash interacted with more warriors, each conversation unraveling layers of the human psyche, duty, and dharma. The war was not just about the clashing of arms but also about the collision of ideologies, beliefs, and inner turmoil's. The Kurukshetra, Yash realized, was as much a battlefield of the mind and soul as it was of warriors.

Chapter 10

The Return and the Revelation

The first light of dawn on the fourteenth day of the war cast long, eerie shadows across the battlefield of Kurukshetra. Yash stood alone amidst the chilling silence, his heart pounding with a mix of fear and excitement. The sight of the battlefield filled him with an indescribable sense of dread and awe. The ground was littered with the bodies of fallen warriors, their lifeless eyes staring into nothingness. The once mighty warriors, who fought with unparalleled valor and honor, now lay still and silent, their tales of bravery forever etched in the annals of time. As Yash looked around, he felt a sense of desolation and loneliness. The absence of Kriyansh, who had been his guide and mentor throughout this journey, was keenly felt. The words of wisdom, the explanations of the intricate philosophy of life and duty, and the soothing presence were all missing. The battlefield seemed to echo his loneliness, intensifying the feeling of desolation. However, as the sun began to rise, casting its warm glow on the devastated battlefield, a familiar figure emerged from the horizon. It was Kriyansh, his face calm and serene. The sight of Kriyansh filled Yash's heart with relief and joy. The sense of loneliness evaporated, replaced by a feeling of comfort and familiarity. "Kriyansh, you're back!" Yash exclaimed, his voice echoing in the vast expanse of the battlefield. Kriyansh gave Yash a gentle smile. "I was always here, Yash. Even when you could not see me, I was with you."

The fourteenth day of the war marked the fall of Dronacharya, the revered teacher and mighty warrior. Dronacharya, who had taught both the Kauravas and the Pandavas, fell to the deceptive tactics of the Pandavas, leading to a significant shift in the tide of the war. Yash watched as the once invincible Dronacharya fell, a sense of disbelief and sorrow filling his heart. Dronacharya had been a symbol of knowledge and power, yet he had chosen the path of unrighteousness, leading to his downfall. The fifteenth day of the war brought with it another major event – the death of Karna. Karna, the son of the sun god, the friend of Duryodhana, and a warrior equal to Arjuna, fell on the battlefield, his body pierced by Arjuna's arrows. Yash watched as Karna, who had lived his life as a charioteer's son despite being a royal prince, fell. His heart filled with sorrow for Karna, who had lived a life of struggle and strife, only to meet his end on the battlefield. As the sixteenth day dawned, Yash found himself reflecting on the events of the past few days. The war was not just a clash of arms; it was a clash of ideologies, of righteousness and unrighteousness, of dharma and adharma. Each warrior, each hero, had a story to tell, a lesson to teach. The war was, in its own way, a reflection of life itself. As the sun set on the sixteenth day, Yash looked forward to the lessons the next days would bring. With Kriyansh by his side, he was ready to face the revelations and the challenges the coming days would bring. His journey had not ended; it had merely reached a crucial juncture. As he stared at the setting sun, Yash knew that he was ready to face the final days of the war, armed with the wisdom and the lessons he had learned so far. As Yash stood on the battlefield, his thoughts turned towards the teachings of Lord Krishna, as told by Kriyansh. He remembered one shloka that had left a deep impact on him:

"Karmanye vadhikaraste ma phaleshu kadachana,"Karmanye vadhikaraste ma phaleshu kadachana,

ma karma-phala-hetur bhur ma te sango 'stv akarmani"ma karma-phala-hetur bhur ma te sango 'stv akarmani"

This verse from the Bhagavad Gita translates to "You have the right to perform your prescribed duties, but you are not entitled to the fruits of your actions. Never consider yourself the cause of the results of your activities, and never be attached to not doing your duty."

This shloka seemed particularly relevant to Yash in the present circumstances. He reflected upon the actions of the warriors on the battlefield. Dronacharya, despite his vast knowledge and wisdom, had sided with the Kauravas, knowing well that they were on the path of adharma. His actions had led to his downfall. Karna, despite being aware of his true lineage, had remained loyal to Duryodhana, choosing friendship over dharma. His loyalty had eventually led to his demise on the battlefield. As Yash pondered over these events, he realized the depth and relevance of Lord Krishna's teachings.

Each of us is responsible for our actions, but we have no control over the outcomes. We can choose to act according to our dharma, without attachment to the results of our actions. The following days of the war brought forth more incidents that underscored this principle. The death of Dushasana at the hands of Bhima, the numerous duels between the great warriors, and the various strategies employed by both sides – all these events were testament to the fact that one's actions inevitably lead to consequences, and that the path of dharma, though difficult, always yields the best results in the end. During this time, Yash also had several interactions with the warriors from both sides. He was moved by their stories, their motivations, and their unwavering commitment to their duties. These interactions provided Yash with a deeper understanding of the complexities of life and the importance of dharma. As the sun set on the sixteenth day, Yash found himself in a reflective mood. The battlefield lay silent, the cacophony of the war replaced by a deafening silence. As he looked at the setting sun, he remembered another verse from the Bhagavad Gita:

"Yada yada hi dharmasya glanir bhavati bharata,"Yada yada hi dharmasya glanir bhavati bharata,

abhyutthanam adharmasya tadatmanam srijamy aham"abhyutthanam adharmasya tadatmanam srijamy aham"

This verse, which translates to "Whenever there is decay of righteousness, O Bharata, and there is exaltation of unrighteousness, then I Myself come forth," reminded Yash of the divine purpose of the war – to restore dharma and vanquish adharma. As the final days of the war approached, Yash knew that he was about to witness history. He was about to witness the triumph of dharma over adharma, of righteousness over unrighteousness. And with Kriyansh by his side, he was ready to understand and assimilate the profound wisdom of these events. The sixteenth day marked the end of another phase of the war, and the beginning of the most critical part. Yash knew that the coming days would bring more challenges, more revelations, and more lessons. But he was ready. With the wisdom of the Bhagavad Gita in his heart and the guidance of Kriyansh, he was prepared to face whatever lay ahead. He was ready to witness the final act of this divine play, the ultimate battle between dharma and adharma.

The seventeenth day of the war dawned with a renewed vigor in the air. Yash could feel the tension, the urgency, and the anticipation of what the day would bring. As the sun rose, casting its first golden rays over the battlefield, he saw the warriors readying themselves for the day's battles. Shields were polished, swords sharpened, and armor fastened. Kriyansh approached Yash; his face serious but calm. "Today, Yash, you will witness the crux of many warriors' destinies. Today's battles will be fierce, and their outcomes will shape the future of this great land."

Yash nodded, his gaze fixed on Shakuni, the crafty uncle of the Kauravas. He had always been intrigued by Shakuni's role in the saga. The man's cunning and strategy had played a significant role in bringing about the war. Yash approached Shakuni, hoping to understand his motivations.

Shakuni looked at Yash with piercing eyes, "Why do you seek me out, observer?"

"I wish to understand," Yash replied, "What drives a man like you? Why the elaborate schemes and the deceit?"

A smirk formed on Shakuni's lips, "For family, for power, for the legacy. I saw the potential in Duryodhana, and I knew with the right guidance, he could rule this land."

"But at what cost?" Yash questioned; his voice filled with genuine curiosity.

"The cost is immaterial when the prize is the throne of Hastinapur," Shakuni responded with a cold intensity.

Yash pondered over Shakuni's words. It was clear that the lure of power and supremacy had clouded Shakuni's judgment, making him prioritize his ambitions over righteousness.

Later that day, Yash witnessed the fierce duel between Sahadeva, the youngest of the Pandavas, and Shakuni. The two warriors clashed with a ferocity that was a sight to behold. Sahadeva, with his skill and righteousness, eventually overcame Shakuni's cunning, putting an end to his malevolent schemes.

As Shakuni lay defeated, Yash approached him once more, "Do you now see the cost of your actions?"

Shakuni, with a pained expression, replied, "I see it now, but it's too late for regrets."

Kriyansh, who had been observing the interaction, commented, "Such is the nature of life, Yash. Sometimes we only realize our missteps when it's too late to rectify them."

The day ended with the Pandavas gaining the upper hand. The Kauravas, though still formidable, seemed to be waning in their resolve.

That night, under the canopy of stars, Yash and Kriyansh sat together, reflecting on the day's events. Kriyansh shared more insights from the Bhagavad Gita, emphasizing the importance of selfless action and righteousness.

Yash, absorbing the teachings, said, "This war, Kriyansh, is not just a physical battle. It's a battle of the soul, of ideologies, of what's right and wrong."

Kriyansh nodded, "Precisely. And as the war nears its conclusion, always remember that it's not the outcome but the journey and the lessons learned that matter."

Yash looked at the vast expanse of the battlefield, the ground bearing witness to the sacrifices and valor of countless warriors. With the wisdom of Kriyansh's teachings and the experiences of the past days, he braced himself for the final chapter of this epic saga.

Chapter 11

The Final Days

The seventeenth day of the war brought with it an aura of dread and anticipation. Yash stood at the edge of the battlefield, his eyes scanning the horizon as the first rays of dawn painted the sky in hues of red and gold. The stars were slowly fading away, making way for the sun. The celestial bodies seemed to align in a peculiar fashion, indicating the rare occurrence of a solar eclipse. There was a palpable tension in the air, a hush before the storm, as if nature itself was holding its breath in anticipation of the impending chaos. The battlefield of Kurukshetra was a sight to behold. The vast expanse of land was dotted with thousands of chariots, elephants, and horses, each ready to charge at a moment's notice. The soldiers of both armies stood tall, their armors glinting in the early morning light, their faces set in grim determination. The war had been raging for sixteen long days, and the once mighty armies of the Pandavas and Kauravas had been reduced to a fraction of their original size. The ground was littered with the bodies of fallen warriors, their dreams and ambitions buried with them in the soil of Kurukshetra. As the sun rose higher in the sky, the battlefield came alive with the sounds of war. The deafening roars of the elephants, the thunderous clashing of weapons, the piercing war cries of the warriors, all filled the air, creating a symphony of chaos and destruction. Amidst all this, Yash stood alone, a solitary figure amidst a sea of warriors. He felt a strange mix of fear and exhilaration. He was a part of this chaos, yet he was detached. He was a participant in this war, yet he was an observer. Suddenly, Yash felt a presence beside him. He turned to find Kriyansh standing there, his face calm, his eyes filled with an inscrutable depth. Yash felt a surge of relief wash over him. He was no longer alone. He had his guide, his mentor with him. "Kriyansh," Yash breathed, his voice filled with relief and joy. "You are here."

Kriyansh merely smiled, his eyes reflecting the calmness of the dawn. "I never left, Yash. I was always here, watching over you."

Yash could only stare at Kriyansh in silent gratitude. His heart felt lighter, the burden of his worries seemed to have lessened. With Kriyansh by his side, Yash felt ready to face whatever the war had in store for him. The seventeenth day of the war was a day of great significance. It was the day when the true extent of the brutality of war was laid bare. The Pandavas and the Kauravas engaged in a fierce battle, their only goal to decimate the other. The rules of war were forgotten, the warriors fought with a ferocity that was both awe-inspiring and terrifying. Despite the intensity of the battle, Yash found himself strangely detached. He watched the battle unfold, the warriors fighting with all their might, the ground getting soaked with the blood of the fallen. He saw the pain and the determination in the eyes of the warriors, their resolve unshaken even in the face of death. He saw the despair in the eyes of the wounded, their dreams of glory shattered. He saw the life slowly ebbing out of the eyes of the dying, their hopes and ambitions fading away with their last breath. The sight of the battlefield filled Yash with a profound sense of sadness. He realized the futility of war, the pointlessness of the violence. He understood that the war was not just a battle for a piece of land or a throne. It was a battle of egos, of unfulfilled ambitions, of deep-seated resentments. It was a war that was fought not just on the battlefield, but also in the hearts and minds of the warriors. As the seventeenth day of the war came to an end, Yash was left with a deep sense of disillusionment. The glamour of war had faded away, revealing the grim reality of death and destruction. He realized the heavy price that was paid for victory, the countless lives that were sacrificed, the dreams that were crushed. He understood that victory in war was not a cause for celebration, but a reason for mourning. With these thoughts in his mind, Yash awaited the dawn of the eighteenth day. The final day of the war was upon them, the day that would decide the fate of the Pandavas and the Kauravas. The day that would bring an end to the violence and bloodshed. The day that would bring closure to the epic saga of the Mahabharata. As Yash stood under the vast expanse of the starlit sky, he couldn't help but feel a sense of anticipation. He knew that the final day of the war would be the most crucial. He knew that the events of the next day would leave a lasting impact on him. And he knew that he was ready to face it all. With Kriyansh by his side, Yash felt a renewed sense of purpose. He knew that he had to witness the end of the war, to see the culmination of the events that he had been a part of. He knew that he had to learn from the war, to take the lessons that it offered, to understand the complexities of life. As Yash looked at the distant horizon, he realized that he had come a long way. From being a confused and aimless youth, he had transformed into a man who understood the complexities of life. He had witnessed the greatest war in history, had seen the rise and fall of great warriors, had learned valuable lessons about life and humanity. He had grown, not just in age, but also in wisdom and understanding. With these thoughts in his mind, Yash awaited the dawn of the final day. He knew that the next day would bring with it the end of the war, but it would also bring a new beginning for him. A beginning of a journey towards understanding life and its intricacies. A journey towards finding his purpose in life. A journey towards self-discovery. And so, under the vast expanse of the starlit sky, Yash stood, a solitary figure amidst the remnants of a great war. His heart was filled with a mix of emotions – sadness for the lives lost, relief for the end of the war, anticipation for the future. But above all, he felt a sense of contentment.

As dawn approached, the air was thick with tension. The battlefield, which had seen countless warriors fall, was eerily calm in the predawn light. The survivors of the sixteen days of combat, weary and bruised, prepared for the last day, knowing that many would not see the sun set.

Yash, now accustomed to the rhythm of war, stood beside Kriyansh, gazing at the Pandava camp. "Kriyansh," he began, "This war... it has changed me. But I still don't understand why such devastation is necessary. Why must brothers kill brothers? Why must friendships be shattered over power?"

Kriyansh looked at Yash, his gaze deep and thoughtful. "War, Yash, is a manifestation of human desires, conflicts, and egos. It's the result of accumulated karma over lifetimes. But remember, every ending also signifies a new beginning. The Mahabharata is not just a tale of war; it's a lesson on dharma, on righteousness." They were interrupted by a sudden commotion. From the Kaurava camp, Shakuni emerged, his face twisted in rage, challenging Sahdev to a duel. The youngest of the Pandava brothers, Sahdev was known for his wisdom and was not as battle-hardened as his siblings. Yash watched intently. This was a different kind of battle, one not of brute strength but of wit and strategy. Shakuni, the mastermind behind the game of dice that had set the stage for the war, was known for his cunning. Sahdev, on the other hand, was known for his righteousness.

The two warriors circled each other, weapons drawn. The atmosphere was tense, with both sides watching in anticipation. Shakuni taunted Sahdev, bringing up the game of dice and the humiliation of Draupadi. Sahdev, calm and composed, responded, “Shakuni, the past is behind us. Today, we fight for the future, for dharma.” The duel was intense. Every strike, every move was calculated. Yash could see the contrast between the two warriors. Where Shakuni’s moves were driven by rage and vengeance, Sahdev’s were driven by duty and honor as the duel reached its climax, Nakul, Sahdev’s twin, unable to bear the sight of his brother in danger, charged at Shakuni. The battlefield erupted in chaos, with warriors from both sides rushing in. The duel had turned into a full-fledged battle. Kriyansh turned to Yash, “Every action has a consequence. The duel was not just between Shakuni and Sahdev; it was between two ideologies, two perspectives of life.” Hours passed, and as the dust settled, Sahdev stood victorious, having defeated Shakuni. However, the victory came at a cost. Many warriors from both sides lay dead or wounded. Yash, deeply affected by the day’s events, turned to Kriyansh, “Is this what victory looks like? At what cost does one claim victory?” Kriyansh, placing a comforting hand on Yash’s shoulder, replied, “Victory and defeat are but two sides of the same coin. It’s the journey, the choices made, and the lessons learned that matter. This war is a testament to the complexities of human nature, the eternal conflict between dharma and adharma."

Night fell on Kurukshetra. The final day of war had concluded, but the lessons it imparted would remain with Yash forever. As he looked at the starry sky, Yash realized that life was not just black and white; it was a myriad of colors, each representing choices, consequences, and lessons. With Kriyansh by his side, Yash prepared to leave the battlefield, his heart heavy yet enlightened. The journey through the Mahabharata had changed him, giving him a new perspective on life, duty, and righteousness. He was ready to embark on a new journey, carrying with him the wisdom of the ages.

Chapter 12

The New Dawn

A surreal quietude hung over the battlefield as the eighteenth day of the war faded into twilight. Yash, standing amidst the desolation of what was once a thriving field of warriors, felt a strange emptiness creep into his heart. The clanging of swords and the battle cries that had filled the air were replaced by a deathly silence, broken only by the occasional whimpers of the wounded and the cawing of the carrion birds circling above. Beside him stood Kriyansh, his face weathered by the horrors of war. The last eighteen days had been a whirlwind of emotions, a torrent of lessons learned and wisdom gained. But now, as the dust settled and the echoes of war began to fade, Yash felt an overwhelming sense of melancholy. The figures strewn across the battlefield were not just bodies; they were stories cut short, dreams unfulfilled, and lives unlived. Turning to Kriyansh, Yash murmured, "Kriy, I want to stay here." His words hung in the air, a testament to the profound transformation he had undergone. The world he knew, the world of deadlines and commitments, seemed trivial compared to the grand tapestry of life and death he had witnessed in Kurukshetra. Kriyansh, wise beyond his years, gazed at Yash with a serene calm. "Yash, this is not our world," he said gently. "We have a life waiting for us. A life that needs us."

A wave of apprehension washed over Yash. Despite the chaos, the battlefield had become a familiar world, and he was not ready to abandon it. But Kriyansh's words echoed in his mind, a gentle reminder of the reality that awaited them. As they journeyed back to their time, Yash felt a strange sense of displacement. He was returning to his world, but he was not the same person. He was leaving behind a part of himself in the battlefield of Kurukshetra, a part that had been touched by the raw reality of life and death. When Yash stepped back into his world, it felt like stepping into a dream. Everything was as he had left it, yet everything had changed. His father was no longer there, his presence replaced by an irreplaceable void. His wife Isha, once distant and indifferent, was now a picture of regret and sorrow. And his dream job at McKinsey was now his reality, a testament to the unpredictability of life. Yet, amidst the whirlwind of changes, Yash found a strange sense of peace. He had travelled through time, witnessed the greatest war in history, and emerged from it with a newfound wisdom. He realized that life was not about running away from challenges, but about facing them with courage. It was not about dwelling on the past, but about living in the present and preparing for the future. As Yash navigated through his life, he held on to the lessons he had learned in Kurukshetra. He remembered the courage of the warriors, the wisdom of Krishna, and the guidance of Kriyansh. He knew that just like the warriors on the battlefield, he too had the power to shape his destiny. Yash's journey was not just a journey through time; it was a journey of transformation, a journey of self-discovery. And as he stepped into the next chapter of his life, he knew that the end of his journey was just the beginning of a new one. The best was yet to come. With the wisdom of the Bhagavad Gita in his heart and the determination to face life's challenges, Yash was ready to embrace the future. He was ready to live his life, not as a mere spectator, but as an active participant. And so, as Yash moved forward, he carried with him not just the memories of the past, but the lessons of the present and the hopes for the future. His journey in Kurukshetra was over, but his journey in life was just beginning. And as the sun set on his past and rose on his future, Yash knew that he was not alone. He had the wisdom of the Bhagavad Gita, the guidance of Kriyansh, and the strength of his experiences to guide him. He was ready to face whatever life had in store for him, ready to embrace his destiny. In the grand scheme of life, Yash had realized, the end was just another beginning. And as he stepped into his new beginning, he knew that the best was yet to come. Yash was ready to embark on his journey, ready to live his life to the fullest. As Yash resumed his regular life, he found himself constantly drawing upon the wisdom he had acquired from Kriyansh and the battlefield of Kurukshetra. Not just in the grand scheme of his existence, but in the minutiae of his everyday life, the teachings became a guiding light. The most significant impact was in his approach to the ongoing POSH case. Rather than letting emotions cloud his judgement, Yash approached it with the rationality and strategic thinking he had observed in the Pandavas. He delved into the evidence, sought truth in testimonies, and approached the case with a newfound sense of duty. His priority was no longer about winning or losing, but about ensuring justice. This shift in perspective had a profound effect on the outcome of the case. With his thoughtful and strategic approach, Yash was able to successfully advocate for the truth and bring justice to the victim. Changes in Yash's life weren't limited to his professional sphere. As he walked down the path of transformation, he distanced himself from his past addictions. His nightly rendezvous with alcohol and drugs, once his escape from reality, now seemed like chains that shackled him to a destructive path. He realized that these were not solutions, but merely illusions that created more problems. Instead of seeking solace in these harmful substances, Yash turned to meditation, just as Kriyansh had taught him. He found that it not only calmed his mind but also gave him the strength to face his issues head-on. He learned to find peace within himself rather than seeking it in external factors. Slowly, but surely, Yash's life began to change. The man who had once been a slave to his habits and circumstances was now the master of his destiny. The teachings from the Bhagavad Gita were not just philosophical musings for him, but practical guidelines that he could apply in his daily life. As Yash navigated through this new phase of life, he realized that the past eighteen days had changed him profoundly. He was no longer the same person who had stumbled upon a strange device and been transported to an ancient battlefield. He had evolved into a wiser, stronger, and more resilient individual, ready to face the challenges that life threw his way. Despite the numerous trials and tribulations, Yash felt a sense of contentment. He had learned to accept life as it was, with its ups and downs, victories and losses, joy, and sorrow. He had learned the importance of duty, of righteousness, and of selfless action. Most importantly, he had learned to live in the present, to cherish each moment, and to make the most of it. With each passing day, Yash felt more and more at peace with himself. He had finally found the balance he had been seeking – the balance between his desires and duties, his dreams and reality, his past and present. He realized that life was not about running away from challenges, but about facing them head-on. As he moved forward, he carried with him not just the memories of the past, but the lessons of the present and the hopes for the future. And as he stepped into this new beginning, he knew that he was ready to face whatever life had in store for him. As Yash started to rebuild his life, he couldn't help but ponder about Kriyansh. There was an air of mystery that still shrouded his friend and guide. Who was Kriyansh really? How did he know so much about the Bhagavad Gita and the events of the Kurukshetra war? These questions nagged at Yash, adding a hint of intrigue to his otherwise ordinary life. One day, while Yash was arranging the study in his home, he stumbled upon the strange device that had sent him back in time. As he picked it up, memories of his incredible journey flashed before his eyes. A wave of nostalgia washed over him, and he was overcome with a strong desire to see Kriyansh again. He felt an inexplicable pull towards the device, a longing for another conversation with his mentor. Suddenly, the device sprung to life, glowing with a bright light. Yash's heart pounded in his chest as he saw a familiar figure materialize in front of him. It was Kriyansh, looking the same as he did on the battlefield of Kurukshetra. "Kriy!" Yash exclaimed, his eyes wide with surprise. "How... why are you here?"

Kriyansh smiled, his calm demeanour a stark contrast to Yash's astonishment. "I thought you might have some questions, Yash," he replied. "And I believe it's time for some answers."

As Yash listened to Kriyansh, he realized the depth of the mystery that surrounded his guide. Kriyansh wasn't just a knowledgeable friend who had guided him in the past; he was a part of a bigger plan, a plan that spanned across time and space. The revelation was shocking, leaving Yash with more questions than answers. But as he looked at Kriyansh, he felt a sense of calm. He knew that no matter how complex or confusing the truth might be, he could face it.

After all, he had faced the horrors of war, the trials of life, and emerged stronger. As the day ended, Yash found himself reflecting on the events of the past few weeks. His life had taken an unexpected turn, leading him down a path he had never imagined. But as he looked back, he couldn't help but feel grateful. For the lessons, the experiences, and most importantly, for Kriyansh. With a newfound sense of purpose, Yash was ready to face his future. He knew that challenges would come, but he also knew that he had the strength and wisdom to overcome them.

As the days turned into weeks, Yash's life began to take on a new shape. The profound lessons he learned from the battlefield of Kurukshetra were not confined to the past but resonated strongly in his present. The teachings of the Bhagavad Gita, once mere words in a sacred text, were now a living philosophy guiding his every action. At work, Yash was no longer the same ambitious young man driven by greed and competition. He approached his projects with a calm resolve, focusing on the importance of duty and the selfless pursuit of excellence. His colleagues noticed a change in him, a new wisdom and humility that set him apart.

His relationship with Isha underwent a transformation as well. The distant indifference that once marked their marriage gave way to a deeper understanding and empathy. They began to communicate openly, appreciating each other's strengths and supporting each other's weaknesses. Their marriage, once on the brink of collapse, was now a partnership of love and respect. Even the city itself seemed to have changed. The once bustling and chaotic streets were now filled with a sense of order and purpose. People seemed kinder, more considerate. The air was cleaner, the noise less jarring. It was as if the world itself had undergone a transformation, reflecting the inner change that Yash had experienced. But the most significant change was within Yash himself. The restless discontent that had once consumed him was gone, replaced by a serene acceptance of life's imperfections. He had found his purpose, his place in the grand scheme of things. He was no longer adrift, but anchored by the wisdom of the Gita and the guidance of Kriyansh.

As Yash continued to navigate his new life, he often found himself reflecting on his incredible journey. The memories of the battlefield, the faces of the warriors, the words of Krishna - all were etched in his mind, a constant reminder of the profound truths he had discovered. But there was one question that still nagged at him, one mystery that remained unsolved. The device that had transported him to the past - what was it? How had it worked? Who had created it? These questions were like a puzzle, pieces of a larger picture that he couldn't quite see.

One day, as Yash was pondering these questions, he received a call from a mysterious scientist named Dr. Aarav Verma. The scientist claimed to have knowledge about the device and requested a meeting with Yash. Intrigued and hopeful for answers, Yash agreed. When they met, Dr. Verma revealed that the device was part of a top-secret project aimed at exploring the possibilities of time travel. It was a prototype, never meant to be used. But somehow, it had found its way into Yash's hands, leading him on a journey that had changed his life.

Dr. Verma was fascinated by Yash's experience and saw it as proof of the incredible potential of the device. But Yash, now wise beyond his years, understood that the device was not just a tool for time travel. It was a portal to wisdom, a gateway to understanding the deepest truths of existence. As they talked, Yash realized that his journey was not just a personal one. It was part of a larger plan, a cosmic design that had brought him to the battlefield of Kurukshetra for a reason. He had been chosen to bear witness to the eternal truths of the Gita, to bring them back to the present and share them with the world. With this realization, Yash knew that his journey was far from over. He had a mission, a purpose that went beyond his personal growth. He was a messenger, a conduit for the timeless wisdom of the Gita.

The device was returned to Dr. Verma, with Yash's promise that it would never be misused. Yash knew that the true power of the device was not in its ability to traverse time but in its ability to reveal the universal truths that transcended time. As Yash walked away from the meeting, he felt a renewed sense of purpose. His journey had brought him full circle, from a lost soul to a man with a mission. He had discovered the truths of life, love, duty, and destiny. And now, he was ready to share them with the world. His relationship with Kriyansh, once confined to the past, continued to thrive in the present. They met often, discussing philosophy, life, and the future. Kriyansh, no longer just a guide, became a friend, a mentor, a part of Yash's life. As the sun set on one chapter and rose on another, Yash knew that he was on the right path. He was ready to face the future, armed with the wisdom of the past. With the Bhagavad Gita in his heart and Kriyansh by his side, Yash was ready to embark on a new journey. A journey not just of self-discovery but of enlightening others. A journey towards a new dawn. The world had changed, and so had he. But the journey was far from over. It was just the beginning. For in the grand scheme of life, the end was indeed just another beginning. And as Yash stepped into his new beginning, he knew that the best was yet to come.

After all, life was not about the destination, but the journey. And Yash's journey was just beginning...

www.ingramcontent.com/pod-product-compliance
Lightning Source LLC
LaVergne TN
LVHW091104150826
845673LV00002B/717